THE ARCHERS
BORCHESTER ECHOES

THE ARCHERS

BORCHESTER ECHOES

Jock Gallagher

BBC BOOKS

*Other titles in
the Archers series*

TO THE VICTOR THE SPOILS
RETURN TO AMBRIDGE

Published by BBC Books
A division of BBC Enterprises Ltd
Woodlands, 80 Wood Lane, London W12 OTT

First published 1988
© Jock Gallagher 1988

ISBN 0 563 20607 1

Set in 10/11 Times Roman by Opus, Oxford
and printed in Great Britain by
Richard Clay Ltd, Bungay, Suffolk

CHAPTER ONE

Oblivious to the shrill clamour of the telephone beside her, Elizabeth Archer gazed dreamily out of the window, watching the rain send shoppers scurrying along the High Street. With less than three months to go, she'd resigned herself to the fact that she wasn't going to be a millionairess by the time she was twenty-one. The commission she earned from selling small ads for the *Borchester Echo* was barely enough to keep her in one glass of champagne a week at Nelson Gabriel's wine bar. Her fall-back idea – marrying into a fortune – didn't look too promising either. She had been going out with Robin Fairbrother on and off for nearly a year but he still seemed a lifetime away from proposing. There was the little matter of his divorce to be settled first.

Elizabeth's instinct for self-preservation finally came to the rescue. Seconds before the wrath of the tele-sales supervisor could descend upon her, she answered the telephone.

"Hello . . . 31746 . . . *Borchester Echo*'s classified advertisement line . . . this is Elizabeth speaking."

Every time she uttered the prescribed phrase she wanted to giggle. It sounded so silly to use her Christian name with complete strangers. She could tell, too, that the callers were slightly unhappy about it. Usually they took a deep breath and stammered a lot before they were able to read out their advertisement – usually but not always.

"Just Elizabeth! I'm not allowed to give my second name."

It was another awkward customer. Whenever it was a man on the line they almost always wanted to know her full name, and some of them were even brave enough to have a go at getting her private phone number. This was one of the brave.

"No, I'm terribly sorry, sir, but I'm not allowed to make exceptions. No, sir, we don't see personal callers at the office. That's a different department. I'm tele-sales and the tele is short for telephone. If you want to hand your advertisement over in person, you should see one of our counter assistants downstairs in the front office. No, sir, I don't take business calls at home."

The harsh click of the receiver being put down told her that another man had woken up to his own silliness. She sensed the brooding presence of Miss Morgan and groaned inwardly. She wasn't one of the supervisor's favourites – mainly, Elizabeth suspected, because she had bullied Jack Woolley, proprietor of the *Borchester Echo*, into giving her the job. He was also the owner of the Grey Gables Country Club in Ambridge, the village where she lived, and she'd known him all her life. In small-town Borchester, having friends in high places appeared to be one of the deadly sins.

"Are we having more difficulty, Miss Archer?"

The royal "we" (and the older woman's sarcastic tone) irritated Elizabeth, but she tried not to show it. Discretion was the better part of something or other. She also needed the job.

"Not really. It was just another heavy breather."

"Don't you think it's a little strange that you're the only one who ever gets that kind of call? I've been taking tele-sales advertisements for more than three years now and I've never had a single person of that nature on the line."

Elizabeth looked up at the thin, drawn face and had to bite her tongue. She wasn't a bit surprised that no one had ever tried to chat up Brenda Morgan. She had a voice to match her appearance – sharp and bitchy – and she used it to keep Elizabeth and the other three tele-ad girls firmly in their place.

Elizabeth had started working in the *Echo* office a year or so earlier. It wasn't exactly the greatest job in the world, but she was very grateful to be earning any money at all. Her attempts to take the fashion world by storm had been a dismal failure. She had set up a partnership with Sophie Barlow to market designer-dresses through a series of fashion events but it had collapsed, despite Sophie's excellent designs, her own business acumen and a hefty slice of financial backing from her mother and Nelson Gabriel. Elizabeth had ended up owing money all over the place and she was still working to pay off the debts, which was the only reason she didn't tell Miss Brenda Morgan exactly what to do with her sarcasm. The telephone rang again and she was saved from further temptation.

This time it was a woman who had several items she wanted to advertise in the "For Sale" column and she expected Elizabeth to give her an expert opinion on how much to ask for a nearly new pram, a drop-side wooden cot in excellent condition, and an assortment of babies' clothes that were, she claimed, quite new. It was the kind of advertisement she hated dealing with. Humdrum domestic matters bored her, but she recognised an opportunity to get a little more commission if she could tease extra words out of the woman. She turned on the charm. It worked, and the end result was a fairly lengthy and expensive ad.

Elizabeth's favourite callers were the people who insisted on using box numbers. She saw them in her usual romantic way as intriguing, shadowy figures who had something they wanted to hide, or a dark secret of some sort. She was able to weave extraordinary fantasies around their possible reasons for wishing to remain anonymous, and her extravagant explanations were a great source of amusement to her colleagues. In the end, Elizabeth had become very interested in the whole question of why some people bought publicity on the one hand and shunned it on the other. She had asked everyone on the paper (and several relatives and friends) how the system of box numbers had started in the first place, but no one had been able to offer any explanation.

The telephone rang again; it was Robin Fairbrother. Elizabeth looked furtively over her shoulder. Brenda

Morgan was busy making one of the other girls' lives a misery.

"Robin, I've told you not to ring me at the office. How did you get my number anyway?"

There was a roar of laughter from the other end of the line.

"It was incredibly difficult – you really ought to give me a prize for ingenuity. I had to find a newsagent's and persuade them to sell me a copy of the *Echo*. I painstakingly searched through the paper until I found the classified advertisement section, followed the instructions to 'ring Elizabeth on 31746', and here I am!"

Elizabeth giggled. She had consistently refused to give Robin a direct office number and had told the switchboard girl not to put him through on her extension because she was already in Miss Morgan's bad books for receiving personal calls. She had forgotten that her photograph and the number were in the paper.

"You are rotten. I'll get it in the neck from the old dragon if she catches me gossiping."

The only sympathy she got was another cheerful laugh.

"Well, I shall have to pretend to be taking down an advertisement, and if Miss Morgan comes along you'll jolly well have to pay for it."

"Come on Elizabeth, you're beginning to sound stuffy. Anyone would think you were as old as me!"

Robin Fairbrother was thirty-four. He was in the wine-trade, and Elizabeth wasn't sure whether she was madly in love with him or simply enjoyed the apparently unlimited supplies of super wine. Either way he was terrific fun. Their relationship had been a bit tricky at first, not only because he had been married before, but also because, quite unbelievably, Robin had turned out to be related to her father's first wife, Grace. He was, in fact, Grace's half-brother. That, Elizabeth had worked out, made Robin her

8

half-uncle-in-law by marriage . . . or something!

When she was first introduced to him the name Fairbrother had rung something of a bell, but she couldn't think why. As Robin had talked about being brought up in Kenya, she had assumed it must have been wishful thinking on her part. It was only later that she discovered how small a world it was.

Robin's father was George Fairbrother, a wealthy businessman who had moved into Ambridge and bought a lot of land in the early 1950s. According to local legend, he'd caused havoc by trying to launch a project to develop ironstone mining. (Elizabeth had no difficulty in imagining the repercussions of such a major project, having seen the way some people in Ambridge had reacted to suggestions that a few houses might be built on a miserable couple of acres at Brookfield.) When George Fairbrother had arrived in the village all those years ago, he'd been a widower with one daughter, Grace. By all accounts, Grace was quite a beauty and had won more than a few hearts before agreeing to marry Elizabeth's father, Phil, then an ambitious young farmer. A few months later, Grace was dead, killed in a terrible fire at Grey Gables Country Club.

Elizabeth had heard the tragic story dozens of times – mainly from Nelson Gabriel, who'd been home on leave from the RAF at the time of the accident – but it still made her want to cry. Grace and Philip Archer had gone to the country club with some friends to celebrate their decision to start a family. Noticing she'd lost an earring, Grace had gone back out to see if she'd dropped it in the car. That's when she had discovered the fire in the stables attached to the club. Her horse, Midnight, was kept there, and she'd rushed in to rescue him. The roof had caved in and she'd been trapped by falling timbers. No one at the club had realised how badly injured she was, but she died in her husband's arms on the way to the hospital.

Philip Archer had eventually recovered from the horror and remarried. But George Fairbrother hadn't ever got over it. Only two years before, he had married again and Robin, Grace's half-brother, was by now a lively toddler. But nothing could take the place of his beautiful daughter and he died not long after, some said of a broken heart. His widow had quickly sold up, and left Ambridge with her baby son Robin to live in Kenya.

When Elizabeth first told her mother – Jill – about Robin, she'd been very upset. She said she didn't want old wounds to be reopened and had refused to let him visit Brookfield. As far as Elizabeth was concerned, it was a perfectly reasonable reaction. She knew how difficult it must have been for her mother to take the place of Grace, the tragic heroine. For once, Elizabeth displayed great tact by taking things very gently until her mother had gradually come round. Robin was now welcome at Brookfield Farm, although it was obvious that neither of her parents were entirely at ease with him. For his part, Robin was the perfect gentleman and never said anything that might create awkwardness.

Now on the telephone it was different. He was teasing Elizabeth, provoking her into a fit of giggles that would ensure the attention of her supervisor.

"Go away, Robin Fairbrother. You're a horrid creature. I don't want to talk to you."

"But I was going to invite you to join me for a glass of champagne after work, Elizabeth."

Robin had no trouble handling her. He knew her weakness.

"Champagne? Ah well, that's different. For two glasses of champagne, I might be prepared to put up with the wrath of Morgan the Gorgon. See you later. Bye."

Elizabeth hung up quickly before Robin could continue the banter. She saw Brenda Morgan coming in her direction and held her breath in anticipation of another telling off. To her surprise, the other woman was smiling.

10

"If you'd like to take a break now, I'll cover for you, Elizabeth."

The reason for this extraordinary change of attitude was soon apparent. Mr Woolley had come into the office and had asked the supervisor if he could have a quick word with Elizabeth. Being obliged to offer Elizabeth a break must have cost Miss Morgan several layers of enamel off her teeth, but she'd do anything to ingratiate herself with the boss.

"Hello, Mr Woolley. Have you come to offer me instant promotion to editor?"

Elizabeth made no bones about wanting to become a journalist, and took every opportunity to press her claim.

"Er . . . well, not exactly, Elizabeth."

Jack Woolley, whose business empire included the Ambridge village stores as well as the *Echo* and the Grey Gables Country Club, wasn't noted for his sense of humour.

"I was just passing and I wondered if you would ask your young man if he could come and see me about some wine I want to order. I hope you don't mind me asking, but I thought he might be pleased if he thought you'd helped him to get a good order. I want quite a lot of wine, you see – for the restaurant as well as for myself."

"Well, I'm not on commission or anything like that, Mr Woolley. At least not yet, but I'll tell him you'd like to see him. When would you like him to call?"

"He can telephone for an appointment any time. If I'm not there Caroline will take a message. By the way, does he do discounts for friends?"

"Friends? I expect he does, but if you're a friend, Mr Woolley, why don't you know his number?"

"I didn't mean that he and I were friends. I just thought that, you know, because of you and me, he might think it appropriate to treat me as a special customer."

Elizabeth enjoyed watching Mr Woolley getting flustered.

11

"Whatever do you mean, Mr Woolley? You're not suggesting that you and I have a special relationship, are you? I mean, I'm very grateful for the job and all that but . . ."

"Good heavens, no, Elizabeth. Gracious me, no. I just meant that me being your employer . . . no . . . no, of course I didn't mean anything more than that."

He had gone purple with embarrassment, as he shot a quick glance around the office to see who might be eavesdropping on the conversation. Elizabeth couldn't keep it up. She giggled.

"Don't worry, I was only teasing."

She liked Jack Woolley. It wasn't his fault that he was one of the *nouveau riche*, and he tried so hard to be a proper country gentleman that it was positively endearing. No one quite knew how he'd made his money, but he was always talking about being a self-made man who'd started life in the back streets of Birmingham.

He had settled in Ambridge more than twenty years ago when he bought the country club. Despite his overt social-climbing, he had eventually gained the affection of most people in the village. He married the widow of the club's previous owner, but she didn't share the general affection for him and walked out after a few years.

Elizabeth had heard rumours that he had once been madly in love with her Aunt Peggy and had actually proposed to her – not that she really believed it. Anyway, whatever the truth, he was still on his own and relied on his personal assistant, Caroline Bone, to enhance his image with her aristocratic background. His greatest moment was when Caroline had somehow arranged for the Duke of Westminster *and* Princess Margaret to visit Grey Gables on the same day. He was always dropping it into conversations. Royal patronage or not, Mr Woolley was never one to spend more than he could help and his constant quest for discounts was almost as notorious as his name-dropping.

"Well, if you could ask Robin to see me, I'd be very grateful."

Elizabeth couldn't resist one final dig.

"How grateful, Mr Woolley? Grateful enough to talk to the editor about giving me a job in the newsroom or on the features page?"

"Now, you know I've told you before that the editor wouldn't take any notice of me if I asked him to give you a job. He's a very independent man, and I don't think it's right for a proprietor to interfere with the way the newspaper is run."

"You should try telling that to Robert Maxwell and Rupert Murdoch. You can hardly say they don't get involved with their papers, and nobody seems to mind that."

"Perhaps not, but I'm not that kind of press baron. I give my editor complete editorial freedom."

"In that case I have to say that I give my 'young man', as you call him, complete commercial freedom to give discounts or not as he sees fit. Sorry, Mr Woolley, but I'm sure you wouldn't want me to misuse my influence, would you?"

Jack Woolley was starting to get cross.

"Now look, Elizabeth, I just thought you might be prepared to do me a very small favour after all I've done for you. However if you feel that you can't help, then you can't help. Let's just forget it."

Elizabeth realised she'd gone too far.

"I'm sorry, Mr Woolley. I was only joking. Of course I'll ask Robin to come and see you. If you give him a big enough order I'm sure he'll offer you a discount. And I really do enjoy working for the *Echo*. I hope I didn't seem ungrateful for the job. It's just that I'd so like to be a journalist, and I know I can do it."

With his feathers unruffled, Jack Woolley became much more amenable.

"You've got to be patient, Elizabeth. I think that's one of the curses of youth – being in a hurry all the time. I happen to know that the editor has been quite impressed with the little bit of writing you've already done. If you just carry on quietly and steadily he might be prepared to let you do some more. I'm not promising anything, mind you. Being a journalist isn't as easy as you seem to think. You need proper qualifications and proper training."

Elizabeth groaned. Her academic career hadn't been exactly brilliant, and she was fed up with being lectured by everybody about her lack of paper qualifications. At boarding school she'd been more interested in the extra-curricular activities such as playing lacrosse, learning the cello, and going to the out-of-bounds local pub! When she'd actually been caught in the pub, the punishment had been immediate expulsion.

She'd gone on to Borchester Technical College with ambitious plans to take A-levels in environmental science and English literature, but again she'd been side-tracked into learning to play the piano and serving on the students' entertainment committee. She'd failed the science exam completely, and only just scraped an E-grade in English literature.

"It's not fair, Mr Woolley. The only reason I don't have the proper certificates is that I'm not very good at sitting exams. I know I can write. I've proved it. You said yourself the editor was pleased. Why should the lack of a silly piece of paper hold me back?"

Jack Woolley looked at his watch.

"I've got to be going now but you know, Elizabeth, I don't think I can afford to buy my wine from Robin Fairbrother if it's going to cost me so much aggravation. I think I'd be better off with my original supplier!"

Elizabeth was contrite.

"Sorry, Mr Woolley, but you can't blame a girl for trying, can you?"

"Goodbye!"

"Bye . . . and of course I'll get Robin to give you a ring."

As Mr Woolley went out, Brenda Morgan's face returned to its normal tight-lipped expression but she somehow managed to resist the sarcastic comments she had on the tip of her tongue. She got up out of Elizabeth's chair without saying anything. The telephone rang again almost immediately, and Elizabeth reluctantly laid aside her journalistic aspirations while she attended to the job in hand. The caller was one of her favourite box number advertisers.

"Hello, Mr Foster. How's the antique business then? What rip-off are you going to perpetrate on the unsuspecting citizens of Borchester this week?"

Alan Foster, a local antique dealer, had been placing small ads in the *Echo* ever since Elizabeth had started the job, and she'd established a cheerful relationship with him. He didn't seem to mind her cheeky comments about the prices he charged.

"Genuine . . . rubbishy . . . sideboard. My word, we are being honest these days, Mr Foster."

There was a minor explosion on the line.

"It's not rubbishy? Oh, Regency! I do beg your pardon. No doubt, if any of our readers are daft enough to respond to this advertisement, you'll be able to provide satisfactory proof of the date you claim for the sideboard's origination? Now, now, there's no need to get over-excited. I've a duty to my customers, you know. I can't just sit by and watch them being conned by dubious characters who hide behind box numbers."

Elizabeth was suddenly aware that the good-natured tone of the conversation had changed. Alan Foster sounded distinctly cool.

"All right, all right, I was only joking. Of course it's a free country and I do realise that it's none of my business why you use box numbers."

A shadow fell across her desk, and she could feel the dragon's breath on her neck. She quickly switched from cheekiness to cool politeness.

"Would you like me to tell you now how much the advertisement will cost? No? Well, if you're sure, I'll have the account prepared for your collection from the

15

front office as usual. Thank you very much for your business, Mr Foster. Goodbye."

Miss Morgan was neither fooled nor impressed, but she said nothing.

Elizabeth looked at her watch. Only another three-quarters of an hour to go. She'd enjoy a glass or two of champagne at Robin Fairbrother's expense, and if they went to Nelson Gabriel's wine bar, she'd be able to ask Nelson a few questions about why a respectable antique dealer should always advertise under a box number. It was very interesting.

CHAPTER TWO

The town hall clock was striking six when Elizabeth put the cover on her typewriter and pulled the telephone jack out of its socket. Another hard day was over and she couldn't wait to get out of the stuffy office. While the other girls vied for the one mirror in the tiny cloakroom, she rushed off to meet Robin Fairbrother. Running down the stairs, she envisaged his bright red Porsche waiting at the kerbside, the engine running and the passenger door open. She'd slip in and they'd roar off to the nearest glass of champagne.

Not this evening.

There was only the rain, and a line of boring boxes on wheels – no Porsche and no Robin. Irritated, she looked at her watch. It was definitely five past six. Any minute now, the rest of the girls would come down from the office and Elizabeth would be subjected to the usual ribbing about being stood up. She wasn't in the mood for that. Pulling up the collar of her coat, she decided to make a dash through the rain to Nelson Gabriel's wine bar about half a mile away in West Street. Robin would know where to find her.

By the time she reached the bar, she was wet through and her hair looked a mess.

"Ah, the wreck of the *Hesperus* has reached port, I see."

The sardonic Mr Gabriel gave no quarter in the battle of insults he constantly waged with Elizabeth. He was also from Ambridge and had known her all her life.

"Hello, Nelson. Can I have a glass of your very finest champagne please?"

The wine bar was deserted and Nelson Gabriel was still not ready for customers.

"You'll forgive me for asking, dear girl, but you are in funds at the moment?"

17

Elizabeth had acquired an unfortunate reputation for always being short of cash.

"Oh, don't be boring, Nelson. I'm supposed to be meeting Robin. He just hasn't turned up yet."

"Supposed to be meeting him? Aren't you sure?"

"Yes, of course I'm sure. He'll be here any minute. I expect he's been held up by the traffic."

Nelson smiled his politest smile.

"Wouldn't it be better – and more ladylike, if I may say so – if we were to wait for the young sir's actual arrival before we open a very expensive bottle of champagne?"

"Honestly, Nelson Gabriel, you can be very unreasonable. You can't expect me to sit around not drinking while we wait for Robin. I told you, he's just stuck in a traffic jam somewhere. He'll be here any minute."

"Then we won't die of thirst while we wait, will we?"

Elizabeth fished in her handbag to see if she had enough money to pay for her drink. She hadn't.

"If you can't trust me until Robin comes, I'll have to pay by cheque, so make it a large champagne cocktail please, barman."

Nelson laughed and shook his head. He knew she had an uncomfortably high overdraft with a very cautious bank manager who certainly wouldn't have given her a cheque card.

"Please, Elizabeth, not me! I've seen too many rubber cheques in my day. Don't let's spoil a beautiful friendship. Be patient. Wait for young Mr Fairbrother. If he said he'd be here, I've no doubt he'll be here shortly. Now if you'll excuse me I must get ready for my *paying* customers!"

Nelson disappeared into the tiny kitchen and storeroom behind the bar and Elizabeth was left to stare out of the window at the rain. Ten minutes later, there was still no sign of Robin. Her impatience had now turned to irritation and was fast becoming anger. Luckily there was still nobody else in the wine bar so no one, apart from Nelson, would know she'd been stood up.

Nelson came out again just as the big clock in nearby Church Square struck half past six.

"Still alone? I'll tell you what, I'll let you have a glass of a simple little wine that seems to suit the less educated taste of some of my clients."

Elizabeth looked appalled.

"Oh, not Spanish plonk!"

Nelson feigned a hurt expression.

"Beggars can't be choosers. I'm offering you a glass on the house, and all you do is throw my hospitality back in my face. Well, I'm not going to force you to drink my wine. By the way, it isn't what you so vulgarly describe as Spanish plonk. It's from Algeria."

Elizabeth realised she was taking her irritation with Robin out on Nelson.

"I'm sorry, Nelson. A glass of Algerian wine would be absolutely wonderful."

It wasn't. Having frequented several wine bars, not to mention countless Young Conservative parties, Elizabeth had drunk dozens of wines of dubious quality, but Nelson's little Algerian number was in a category all of its own. After two sips she felt as if her teeth were about to drop out.

"Well?"

Nelson stood beside her, waiting for her reaction.

"Interesting. Very interesting. I think it would make a really first-class paint-stripper. Have you tried marketing it in the do-it-yourself shops?"

Nelson smiled.

"It is a trifle immature. I wouldn't normally be selling it at this stage in the evening. I usually keep it for later when the customers' palates are a little jaded."

There were no other palates around, jaded or otherwise, and Elizabeth suddenly remembered that she wanted to ask Nelson about Alan Foster, the mysterious antique dealer.

"Nelson, do you know a man called Alan Foster? He runs an antique business."

19

Nelson frowned.

"That's not a name I recall. He must be new to the area. Where's his shop? In Borchester or one of the villages?"

"Well, that's just it. He doesn't seem to have a shop or anything like that. He only uses box numbers."

"Slow down, Elizabeth, you're losing me. This man is a dealer but he doesn't have a shop? Does he work from home perhaps?"

"I didn't think of that."

"It's fairly common practice in the antiques world, you know. Many dealers think good furniture is best shown in a more domestic setting."

"But why should he always insist on using box numbers?"

Nelson looked puzzled.

"That I can't explain, dear girl. It does sound a trifle unusual."

"Do you think it sounds a bit shady, Nelson?"

"The word I used, dear girl, was 'unusual'. As someone who has suffered from such inaccurate descriptions, I wouldn't dream of impugning this man's character without knowing all the facts."

Elizabeth had heard dozens of stories about Nelson over the years, but she had never stopped to wonder whether any of them could be true. That was before her journalistic ambitions had surfaced. Now she suddenly saw the enigmatic Mr Gabriel as a possible subject for an *Echo* profile. She could already see the headline: "Gabriel was no Angel".

"I don't suppose you would like the opportunity to set the record straight, would you? If you gave me all the dirt . . . I mean, all the facts, I could do a great piece on you in the paper."

Nelson looked affronted.

"There's no record to be put straight, and if there was I'd hardly choose to do it in the local rag. In any case, my understanding of your role on the newspaper is that you're in the classified advertisements department, and very pretty you look in that picture of you holding the telephone!"

"That's only a temporary arrangement until they can find a vacancy for me on the reporting staff."

Nelson was about to make another cutting retort when the door opened. To Elizabeth's disappointment, it wasn't Robin but a bedraggled and windswept young couple.

While they were being attended to, she started mentally working out how much she already knew about Nelson. Quite a lot really, but how much of it would be printable? She knew, for example, that he had been tied up with a mail robbery at some point and had been on the run from Interpol. That would make terrific copy. He'd eventually been arrested and put in gaol, but then he had been acquitted at the trial. Most people said he'd been lucky to get away with it. Only his father, dear old Walter Gabriel, had protested his innocence.

Elizabeth's butterfly mind fluttered on. What a wonderful subject Walter would make! Maybe she could persuade the editor to give her a weekly column that she could fill with pen portraits of the district's characters. Walter Gabriel would certainly qualify. He'd been one of Ambridge's eccentrics for as long as anyone could remember. He was well over ninety, but still managed to look after himself in Honeysuckle Cottage.

She liked talking to him because he was always so funny. He'd been a good friend of her grandfather's so she knew that at least some of his tales were true because she'd heard them from her own family too. He'd had his own small farm at some stage, but when his wife died he'd let it run down and then sold up. That was about thirty years ago and since then he'd played havoc in Ambridge with a whole string of entrepreneurial ventures that had left the villagers variously bemused, bothered and bewildered.

Elizabeth remembered her grandmother telling her about Walter's exploits as the local bus operator. He'd bought one of the country's first mini-buses, and seemed to be doing quite well until he decided that there was also money to be made out of transporting livestock. His mistake was to use the same bus for passengers and pigs. Neither side had seemed happy with the arrangement!

It was Walter himself who'd told her about the time he went into partnership in a Borchester pet shop. He'd so enjoyed being back among animals he'd decided to set up a fairground sideshow with elephants and seals. Elizabeth suddenly found herself laughing out loud as she remembered old Walter's hilarious tales about the elephants, Tiny Tim and Rosie, and the seals, Mutt and Jeff. It made today's Ambridge seem very dull and boring.

The young couple, who were still the only other customers, looked across in surprise and Nelson rejoined her with an anxious look on his face.

"I hope it isn't my Algerian wine that's had this effect on you. I can't afford another scandal. I'm only just recovering from the loss I made on buying that Austrian shipment that everyone thought had been doctored with anti-freeze."

Elizabeth fought to control her laughter.

"As a matter of fact, Nelson, I was thinking about your father."

"I'm glad you find him amusing. Some people have more respect for the elderly."

"Don't be silly, Nelson, I wasn't being disrespectful. I was thinking how fascinating my readers . . ."

"*Your* readers?"

"Oh, all right then, the *Echo* readers . . . how interesting they would find your father's exploits over the years and I suddenly remembered his story about the elephants."

Elizabeth had another fit of giggles. The young couple finished their drinks and left. Nelson watched them go and turned on Elizabeth.

"Now look what you've done. You've driven my only clients away, and on a night like this I'm not likely to get too many more. I hope you and young Mr Fairbrother will drink enough to make up my losses. Where is your champagne Charlie friend anyway? You've been here three-quarters of an hour. He is coming, isn't he?"

Elizabeth looked at her watch. It was almost seven and she felt a strange mixture of anger and embarrassment. She tried to hide both from Nelson.

"Oh, who cares whether it's tonight or tomorrow night that I was supposed to see him? I'm beginning to enjoy your Algerian wine, and in the meantime you and I can talk about this profile I'm going to do for the paper."

Nelson looked at the almost empty bottle and poured the remains into Elizabeth's glass.

"That, my dear girl, is the last of the wine, and it's all you're getting from me this evening. As a man of indeterminate years I have no wish to see the details of my life blazoned in the press."

Elizabeth had a pretty good idea of his age. She knew he'd done his National Service in the RAF, starting in 1951, the Festival of Britain year. He must have been eighteen then, so that made him about fifty-five or fifty-six.

"Of course, I don't really need to have an interview. I could do a story from our cuttings and all the gossip I've heard about you in Ambridge. The big boys in Fleet Street and Wapping do that all the time. Mind you, there's no telling how accurate it would be. It would be so much safer getting it from the horse's mouth."

Nelson was unmoved by the threat.

"I might remind you that the big boys, as you call them, also pay out substantial sums in libel damages. I hardly think our friend Jack Woolley would be very happy if you landed him in the courtroom to be stripped of that self-made money."

"Oh, don't be a spoilsport, Nelson. I need a good story. My career is at stake. If I don't persuade the editor that I can be as good a reporter as Alastair Wilson or Helen Stevenson, I'll be stuck in tele-sales for the next forty years."

Elizabeth suffered from the arrogance of youth in believing that the world owed her a living, but Nelson didn't see himself as having any such responsibility.

"You do seem to have a problem. Why not pursue the luckless Mr Foster? He seems to have more of a story to tell than I do. I've led a blameless life, the details of which would have you and your readers bored rigid.

"For example: I was born and brought up in Ambridge and never set foot outside the village until I went into the air force. I was too mediocre to make air crew and spent the first two years as a minor bureaucrat in a very large unit. My good behaviour won me promotion to corporal and I allowed myself to be talked into signing on as a regular. I was bribed by the three stripes of the sergeant's rank and served out the remaining eight years without further distinction. Are you bored yet?"

Elizabeth shook her head.

"Hurry up and get on to the juicy bits."

Nelson looked at her sadly.

"But I've told you already, there are no juicy bits. That's it. I came out of the air force, took a few jobs and dabbled in the odd business venture until I worked the restlessness out of my system. I came back to dear old Borsetshire, settled down and . . . well, as they say in your trade, the rest is history."

Elizabeth looked at him in amazement.

"You've missed out all the interesting bits. I mean, what about being in gaol? What was it like being an armed robber?"

She hadn't meant to mention the robbery so early on and she looked at Nelson apprehensively to see if she had upset him. He didn't look cross.

"Ah, the great mail robbery . . . that's what you're after, is it? Now I *am* going to disappoint you. I'll tell you the whole story and you'll see how uninteresting it really is. It was all a misunderstanding, and if you read your cuttings you'll see that the judge must have agreed with me because I was acquitted."

"But I thought everyone said you went to prison?"

"So I did, but only on remand while the court hearing was being sorted out. That was part of the mix-up."

Nelson fell silent and started polishing glasses behind the bar.

"Well?"

"Well, what?"

Elizabeth could scarcely contain herself.

"You haven't told me anything. You said you were going to tell me the whole story. What was the mix-up?"

"Did I say mix-up? Perhaps that's because I'm much too polite to use the correct phrase in the company of a young lady. Anyway, I've changed my mind. I don't want the *Borchester Echo* raking over old coals. I know who'd be the one to get burnt: me!"

Elizabeth's curiosity was much stronger than her journalistic ambition.

"Don't be silly, Nelson. I wouldn't dream of printing anything you didn't want published. I don't want to be that kind of ruthless reporter. On a local paper like ours you have to earn the trust and respect of the community you serve and you can only do that by being honest and fair-minded. That's what Keith Parker, the editor, told me the other day."

Nelson could feel another of Elizabeth's lectures coming on. Whenever she had a bee in her bonnet about blood sports, vegetarianism or any one of a dozen other subjects, she had a tendency to harangue anyone prepared to listen.

"You're beginning to sound like defence counsel for freedom of the press!"

Elizabeth was suitably abashed.

"Let's talk off the record, then."

"Off the record?"

"Yes, that means I won't be able to report anything you say."

"You don't mean we could have a normal conversation, do you?"

"Oh, Nelson, stop it. You're teasing me. Of course that's what I mean. You've got me all agog about this robbery thing. Please go on. Please."

The incident she was referring to had happened twenty years earlier, almost to the day, Nelson reflected.

"You might not believe it, but your cousin Jennifer was one of the main causes."

"Jennifer?"

Elizabeth had heard several stories about her cousin but none of them had included a love affair with Nelson Gabriel. She couldn't believe it.

"Not Cousin Jennifer?"

"Yes, the same Mrs Aldridge in whose mouth butter wouldn't melt nowadays. She was a very pretty girl when she was twenty-one, and I made the mistake of falling hopelessly in love with her. We were close for quite some time. That was how I became financially involved with her father."

"You were in business with Uncle Jack? I thought he was hopeless with money. Didn't he drink heavily and gamble a lot?"

Nelson ignored her interruption.

"He invested some money in a casino and betting shop company that I owned at the time. Sadly, my relationship with Jennifer went wrong at about the same time as the company began to fail. At that point, I hadn't even realised that Jennifer was seeing another man, so you can imagine how shocked I was when I discovered that she was going to have a baby. Most people tried to put the blame on me, but she and I knew that wasn't true. I was devastated. With the business going downhill as well, I couldn't take any more. I left the country."

Elizabeth looked at him in amazement. He seemed much too cool a customer to run away because of a woman. She listened with renewed interest as the story unfolded.

"What I didn't know was that some months later, I was reported missing after a plane crash in France. I should have been on the plane, but I'd changed my mind about coming back to Britain at the last minute and decided to go native on the Riviera for a while."

Elizabeth was listening intently, but she couldn't help interrupting again.

"I thought you *had* been on the plane, but had managed to parachute to safety. Wasn't the pilot supposed to have sent your father some money and a letter in your handwriting?"

Nelson laughed.

"I've heard that tale too, but I assure you there's absolutely no truth in it. I told you the facts would be boring."

"Didn't you know that your father and everyone in Ambridge had been told that you were dead?"

"No, I didn't. The way I was feeling about Jennifer Archer, Ambridge was not my favourite place, and I'm sorry to say that at the time I even regarded my own father as part of the conspiracy to make me miserable.

"I fell in with some pretty rough characters in the south of France. None of us had much money and we got around to talking about the easiest way of getting some. I promise you it seemed like a joke at first – the idea of staging a robbery – and I entered into the fun of things by exaggerating the amount I knew about the movement of mail vans in Borsetshire.

"Before I realised it, the whole operation had turned serious and I found myself being called 'Boss' by the other men."

Elizabeth stifled a giggle but Nelson didn't seem to notice.

"I was pretty fed up with life in general, and in the end I couldn't think of any good reason for not going ahead with it."

To Elizabeth's frustration, a crowd of customers came into the wine bar and Nelson had to break off to serve them. Watching him behind the bar, she couldn't imagine him mixing with crooks. With his silver hair, neat business suit and impeccable manners, he looked more like a pillar of society than an ex-gangster. She couldn't really see him as Jennifer Aldridge's lover either. Nelson was right about Jennifer's image these days – it was one of total respectability.

Elizabeth had never said it out loud, but she really didn't much like her cousin. In some ways it was a case of sour grapes. Jennifer had her own weekly column in the *Echo*, and no one could understand why. Her writing was stiff and usually rather dull. Earlier in the year, Keith Parker had agreed that Elizabeth could take over for a week while Jennifer was away, but it hadn't worked out because Jennifer had cancelled her holiday. Then Elizabeth had been allowed to write some pieces about restaurants, but when people said how good they were, Jennifer had given the impression that she'd written them herself. Elizabeth had got her own back by writing a scathing piece about Jack Woolley's restaurant at Grey Gables . . . for which she had still not been forgiven!

It wasn't only professional jealousy that irked Elizabeth, however. It was also what she saw as Jennifer's hypocritical attitude. Everyone knew about the sordid episode of the illegitimate child. It had turned out that her secret lover had been the Irish barman in her father's pub, and he'd disappeared at the first sign of trouble. Despite her murky past, Jennifer still put on all sorts of airs and graces. She'd also reacted very badly when her husband Brian had been caught having a fling with Caroline Bone. Instead of taking it out on her errant husband, she'd vented all her anger on poor Caroline, and had managed to make herself look silly . . . not the best situation for a journalist to find herself in, thought Elizabeth.

"Sorry about the interruption, but I'm sure you understand that my livelihood must come before my boring life story."

Nelson had finished serving the group of customers and was in the process of opening another bottle of wine. It wasn't Algerian. Confesssion seemed to be good for his soul.

"Where did I get to?"

Elizabeth glanced at the people drinking at the other end of the bar, but Nelson seemed unconcerned about the risk of being overheard.

"You were telling me about how bitter and twisted you were feeling."

"Oh, yes. Well, the crowd I'd met in France all came back to England and we rented the old Paunton Farm just outside Ambridge, and that's when I suddenly realised what I was doing. You can imagine how frightened I was. I'm not a crook at heart, you know. I may have been . . . er . . . a bit of a rogue in my younger days, but a villain I most decidedly am not. I suppose a cynic like you would put it down to mere cowardice. Certainly, it did enter my head that I might get hurt during the operation. But I was also concerned about innocent bystanders. I tried to talk the others out of it, but when it became clear that I was wasting my time I packed my bags and left."

Elizabeth looked disappointed.

"So you weren't actually involved with the robbery?"

"Sorry to disappoint you, but no. I left long before. Unfortunately the police found my fingerprints at the farmhouse. They put two and two together and made five. I knew Interpol were after me but I was able to keep one step ahead of them for more than two months."

"Why didn't you give yourself up?"

"I was much too scared to do that. Don't forget, I had been central to the planning of the robbery, and I knew that would make me as guilty as any of those who had taken part in it."

Elizabeth was puzzled.

"Did it make you an accessory before the fact or something?"

Nelson nodded his head and looked grave.

"It would have made me a lot of things – all of them decidedly nasty – if I hadn't had such a good barrister. When he had finished pleading my case even I believed I was innocent. The jury found me not guilty and I was acquitted."

Elizabeth nodded regretfully.

"You were right. It won't make a very good story. I don't think many people would be very interested in a man who was *nearly* a robber. If you're not prepared to embroider things a bit more than that, you'll just have to help me check up on Alan Foster. Let's hope he's a *real* crook."

CHAPTER THREE

The next morning Elizabeth couldn't make up her mind whether to be worried about Robin or just angry with him. He hadn't turned up at Nelson's and he hadn't rung her to make any kind of apology or excuse. She made up her mind: she was cross. It would be quite soon enough to be sorry if she heard later that he'd had an accident or something.

Luckily the telephone had been ringing almost non-stop so she hadn't had much time to think about him. But now she was beginning to seethe. She'd had to beg a lift home from Nelson and that had meant waiting until closing time. The wine bar had temporarily stopped providing food and she'd drunk rather a lot of wine. Admittedly, she had been a bit squiffy by the time she'd got back to Brookfield, and her father had read her the riot act for being so late and making so much noise. Didn't she realise that farmers had to be up at the crack of dawn? And so on, and so on. Damn Robin Fairbrother. She'd have a few choice words for him . . . if he ever bothered to contact her again.

Meanwhile, she wasn't feeling too bright this morning. It wasn't exactly a hangover she was suffering from, although she probably deserved one. She just felt dull, and probably a bit deflated because yet another idea for breaking into journalism had gone out of the window with Nelson Gabriel's boring revelations about his so-called shady past. And Brenda Morgan could always be relied on to make matters worse.

"This advertisement doesn't make sense. You've messed it up from start to finish, and you haven't bothered to take the customer's telephone number so we can't ring them back to correct it."

Elizabeth tried to look apologetic, but Miss Morgan continued.

"It simply isn't good enough. If you don't pull your socks up I'll have to consider taking you off the phones and putting you on accounts."

That was the ultimate punishment at the *Echo*, and Elizabeth groaned inwardly. She looked at the paper Brenda Morgan had thrust in front of her. It was a mess. It wasn't the first time she'd let her mind wander, and she was sure the supervisor had been counting the number of mistakes she'd made over the past few months. It looked as if the accounts department would soon have another reluctant debutante, but she had one last ploy up her sleeve.

"You're right, Miss Morgan. It is awful. I've got no excuse. I shouldn't let my personal affairs affect my work. I realise I'm very lucky to have a job at all and . . ."

Brenda Morgan interrupted her, just as Elizabeth had hoped.

"What's the matter? You're not having trouble with that boyfriend of yours again, are you?"

The supervisor suffered from a combination of nosiness and the mother-hen syndrome. She was desperate for the girls to confide in her. She always wanted to hear details of their love lives and they reckoned it was because she was sex-starved herself. This morning Elizabeth was happy to satisfy her curiosity.

"Yes, I'm afraid so. But I know that's no excuse for being slapdash with my work. I am sorry, Miss Morgan."

The older woman looked at her with what seemed to be compassion.

"Now, I've told you before, Elizabeth. You must call me Brenda. I'm a friend as well as your boss."

Elizabeth almost burst out laughing. The thought of being friends with anyone called Brenda, let alone this particular Brenda, was hysterically funny. However, visions of becoming an accounts clerk helped her control herself, as the supervisor became even more solicitous.

"Put your calls on to the answering machine and have a cup of coffee with me. You can tell me all your troubles – it will help you get them off your chest."

Elizabeth had heard about similar sessions with the other girls, but this was her first time, and she had no idea what to say as she was led into the tiny staff room.

"Now, dear, you sit down and relax while I put the kettle on."

In the few minutes it took Brenda Morgan to make the coffee, Elizabeth had worked out a story to make her boss feel like a real confidante.

"My boyfriend's had an accident."

"Is he badly hurt?"

"Well, that's the trouble. I don't know. He's in hospital and they won't give information to anyone except a relative over the telephone."

Brenda Morgan's interest was already waning.

"Why don't you go to the hospital at visiting time? They'll let you in then."

Elizabeth played her trump card.

"I can't do that either. His wife might be there, and that would cause a terrible scene."

Brenda's sharp intake of breath was all Elizabeth needed to hear to know that she had hooked her victim.

"His wife? Elizabeth, you haven't been going out with a married man, have you?"

Elizabeth tried to look shamefaced.

"Um . . . er . . . well, yes. I'm afraid I have, but honestly, Brenda, I didn't know he was married when we started going out."

Brenda Morgan's fascination easily outweighed her initial shock.

"How long has this been going on, Elizabeth? Do your parents know about it? What about his wife? Does she know?"

Elizabeth was now in deeper than she had intended. Fibs were going to have to be supplanted by lies.

"No. Nobody knows. I haven't been able to talk to anyone about it. I feel so ashamed. Please don't tell anyone!"

She knew it would only be a matter of minutes before Jenny Hinds, Ann Jensen and Liz Cole – the other tele-ad girls – were subjected to a blow-by-blow account of the conversation.

"You can rely on me, Elizabeth. I shan't say a word to a soul. You can tell me anything in complete confidence. That's one of the responsibilities of being in my position. But tell me, how serious are things between you and this man? Have you . . . er . . ."

Elizabeth knew what was coming next and decided enough was enough.

"Look, Brenda, I'm really very grateful for your kindness. You've been a great help, and I feel much better now that I've been able to talk to someone. But I'd better get back to the phones. Thank you very much."

Brenda Morgan was frustrated. There was so much more she wanted to know about this shocking affair with a married man. Elizabeth Archer wasn't even twenty-one yet. It was disgusting.

When Elizabeth went back into the main office, Jenny Hinds beckoned her over, and furtively passed her a note. It was like being back at school. Sitting at her own desk with her headphones on but not plugged in, Elizabeth looked at the note written on a tele-ad form with one word in each box as prescribed by the printers.

"Mr/Fairbrother/wine-merchant/called./Has/urgent/business/to/discuss./Can/you/ring/him?/Says/you/know/number./Sounds/dishy./Is/he/the/red/Porsche?/"

Elizabeth looked across at Jenny, smiled her appreciation, and nodded in answer to her question. Jenny was the nicest of the girls in the office and the only one who would break the Morgan rules about personal calls and messages. The tele-ad phones had been doctored so that they couldn't be used for outgoing calls. If there was ever any problem that might mean ringing a customer back to query the wording of an ad, the unfortunate tele-ad girl had to confess her sins to Miss Morgan and get permission to use the one phone in the office with an outside line. After her far-from-cosy little *tête-à-tête*, there was no way Elizabeth could get access to that this morning. Robin would have to wait until lunchtime.

She plugged in her headphones and picked up a call almost immediately.

"This is Brendan Cahill. I'm Alan Foster's partner. Can I place a couple of ads, please?"

Elizabeth perked up at once. She knew there had to be a story in a shadowy antique dealer with a partner called Brendan Cahill.

"Certainly, Mr Cahill. Can I have your address and telephone number please?"

"Now, there's no need for such formality. Sure, didn't Mr Foster tell me he had an arrangement with you? You take the ads, and he drops in to pay the enormous bill the next time he's passing your office."

Elizabeth felt thwarted, but even more intrigued. She'd hoped to tease at least a telephone number out of this Brendan Cahill, but if even he was being so cagey there had to be something fishy going on. She decided to probe from a different angle.

"We're carrying out a survey at the moment, Mr Cahill, on the success rate amongst advertisers who use the *Borchester Echo*. I wonder if I could ask you a few questions."

There were no flies on Alan Foster's partner.

"Questions? Glory be, girl. Sure, we've got a business to run and not enough time to breathe, let alone be after doing Jack Woolley's work for him. We're more than happy with the replies we get so if you'll forgive me, darling girl, I'll be off before the hordes descend upon us. Good day to you!"

He rang off and Elizabeth was left in a state of helpless frustration. Her journalistic instinct – and it

35

was no good anyone telling her it was just plain nosiness – told her that there was a good story in Messrs Foster and Cahill. She'd get to the bottom of it somehow. The problem was that her journalistic instinct and her journalistic experience didn't always match up. Her thoughts were interrupted by another call. It was Robin Fairbrother.

"Elizabeth, I'm sorry about last night. I got caught up with some business clients and simply couldn't get away."

Elizabeth thought that was a pathetic excuse, but with Brenda Morgan hovering somewhere in the background she couldn't say what she felt like saying. Instead she turned on her coolest, most businesslike voice.

"We run the telephone service to make things as convenient as possible for busy people like you, sir."

Robin got the message.

"I couldn't ring you. I didn't know where you were."

"We're here from nine o'clock in the morning until six o'clock in the evening, sir."

"But, Elizabeth, it was after six before I realised I wasn't going to be able to make it."

By now Elizabeth was really angry. Their date had been for six so he'd have been late anyway. He also knew that she would almost certainly have gone to the wine bar. He could have rung her there. Failing that, he could have got her at home.

"I'm terribly sorry, sir, we have fixed rates for our advertisements. If you can't afford them, I'm afraid there's nothing I can do for you. Thank you for calling anyway. Goodbye."

She flicked the cut-off switch before Robin could offer any further explanation. She was fed up with his excuses. He had let her down several times in the time she had known him, and it was usually his wife who caused the problem by making some last-minute demand or threat. It seemed that she couldn't accept the separation. Elizabeth sighed wearily and decided nothing would ever come of her relationship with Robin. She wondered if they could even go on being good friends.

"What are you doing for lunch, Elizabeth?"

It was Helen Stevenson from the editorial department. Elizabeth looked at her watch.

"Gosh, is it lunchtime already? Doesn't time fly when you're having fun?"

Helen smiled. She was much older than Elizabeth, but she liked the younger girl's sharp sense of humour. She was always good company.

"If you're not having lunch with one of your dashing young men, I thought we might drop in to one of the pubs on the other side of town for a change. I don't think I can stand the sparkling repartee of my male chauvinist colleagues today."

Elizabeth felt herself blushing. There was nothing she would rather have done than go off with Helen and talk about being a journalist, but she didn't have any money.

"I'm awfully sorry, Helen, but this is another of my broke days. I wasn't going to have lunch. I was just going to wander around the shops to see what else I couldn't afford."

Helen laughed.

"Come on, don't be silly. You can be my guest. We can't have members of the *Borchester Echo* staff suffering from malnutrition. I think I can just about afford two ploughman's lunches on the miserable pittance Jack Woolley pays me!"

When they got to the lounge bar of the Horse and Jockey, the two girls settled themselves at a corner table and Helen went off to get the drinks. She brought back two gin and tonics.

"I don't normally drink gin at lunchtime, but I've had a rotten morning and I reckon I've earned this."

Elizabeth nodded in agreement.

"I've had one of those days as well, but as you're buying the drinks, it's your turn to complain first!"

Helen smiled, and realised again why she had sought out young Elizabeth Archer to relax with.

"It's those men in the newsroom. They're so bloody arrogant. I've been working in weekly newspapers for nearly fifteen years and they still treat me like a junior reporter – just because I'm a woman."

Elizabeth looked sympathetic. The farming world was the same. At home, her brother and father behaved as if she were the village idiot when it came to discussing agriculture.

"What have they been doing to you today?"

Helen shook her head.

"It's what they haven't been doing that's annoyed me so much. I think there's a very good story in the uncertainty over land prices and the effect it's having on farmers but when I tried to sell them the idea for a feature, they said I couldn't do it because it would cut across the agricultural correspondent."

Elizabeth looked surprised.

"I didn't know we had an agricultural correspondent. Who is he?"

Helen flushed angrily.

"That's just it, we don't. There was some old boy called Arnold Thomas who used to do farming pieces for the paper for donkey's years, and he always regarded himself as the agricultural expert. He was on some kind of retainer – probably next to nothing if my salary is anything to go by. I tried to ring him this morning, and discovered that the poor old soul had been dead for three years. That gives you some idea of when we last carried anything important about agricultural affairs, and there are more people living in the countryside around Borchester than there are in the town."

Elizabeth could see Helen's frustration building up again.

"What did they say when you told them that Arnold Thomas had died?"

"They told me I'd have to wait until they appointed a new correspondent so I could clear my story with him. 'Him' mind you. Not the faintest possibility that it could ever be a 'she' writing about farming!"

Elizabeth could picture the scene only too well. The ancient features editor, Campbell Lowrie, leaning back on his equally ancient chair and looking at Helen over the top of his specs, shaking his head sadly and complaining about the cruelty of a life that brought him only idiots to try to turn into craftsmen. To Lowrie, a Scotsman brought up as a Calvinist, women automatically fell into the idiot category. One day, Elizabeth vowed, she would tackle him on whether or not his mother was an idiot and if so, what did that make him?

"When are they going to appoint a new man?"

Helen downed the remainder of her gin and tonic before answering.

"I doubt if they'll bother. They've managed for the past three years without one, and I suspect they'd find it hard to persuade our beloved proprietor to part with more money for a new post."

As Helen went to the bar to buy another two drinks, Elizabeth began to see a glimmer of hope for her own aspirations.

"If they did advertise, would you be interested in the job, Helen?"

The older girl almost spluttered.

"Of course I'd be interested, but they probably wouldn't even let me apply. They've made it clear that it's a male domain."

Elizabeth was already plotting to waylay Jack Woolley and warn him about the dangers of treating women as anything less than equals. She didn't know what the Equal Opportunities legislation laid down, but it was a safe bet that Jack wouldn't know either. If she could persuade him that Helen would make an excellent agricultural correspondent, a vacancy would be left for a general features writer and reporter. At this point she remembered that she hadn't relayed

Jack's message to Robin. She'd have to remedy that without delay. She looked at her watch. With luck, Robin would be in his office.

"Helen, I'm terrribly sorry, but I really do have to fly back to the office before the dragon sentences me to the accounts department for life. Why don't you come home to Brookfield with me for supper tonight and we can finish our conversation then?"

Helen shook her head sadly.

"Not tonight, I'm afraid. I've got to cook dinner for James and a mob of his precious friends from the studio."

James was Helen's husband. He was a television producer in Birmingham. Elizabeth had met him once and he'd seemed like an absolute charmer, but from what she'd heard about the glamorous end of the media she guessed that some of his friends were not quite so nice. Poor Helen. It seemed as if her bad day wasn't over yet.

"What about tomorrow night then? Bring James and let him see how the other half live."

"I think he'll probably be working late tomorrow. He usually stays late if he's not entertaining at home, but I'd love to come."

"It's a date! But now I must scoot. Thanks ever so much for lunch. It's very sweet of you to pay. You stay and have another drink. I think you deserve it."

Helen didn't disagree and Elizabeth left her winding her way to the bar again.

Outside, she made a beeline for the nearest telephone kiosk. It was out of order. So was the second one, and the third. By the time she found one that would accept her money, she was getting perilously close to Brenda Morgan's boiling point, but she'd have to take the risk. Doing a favour for Jack Woolley was vital to the success of her strategy and she'd already forgotten that she was supposed to be angry with Robin. When someone eventually answered, it was a girl who said Mr Fairbrother was still at lunch. Elizabeth was exasperated.

"Well, could you take a message for him, please? It's very important. Tell him it could mean a lot of very good business. Ask him if he could ring Mr Jack Woolley at the Grey Gables Country Club in Ambridge . . . no, not Cambridge . . . Ambridge . . . just outside Borchester. Tell him it's about supplying wine, lots of wine . . . yes, in bottles. Tell him to say it was Elizabeth Archer who asked him to call . . . A.R.C.H.E.R."

By the time she had finished, Elizabeth felt exhausted. She hoped she never sounded so gormless on the telephone and she made a mental note to be twice as pleasant to callers in future. As she turned the corner towards the *Echo* office, she saw a red Porsche parked on double yellow lines and the friendly neighbourhood traffic warden slowly and painstakingly writing out a parking ticket. There was no sign of Robin. Elizabeth groaned. If he had gone upstairs to the tele-ads department and fallen into the hands of Brenda Morgan, her whole intricate story would be shot through.

Upstairs, her worst fears were confirmed. Robin, armed with a huge bunch of flowers, was talking confidentially to the supervisor. There was something suspicious going on. She was smiling. As Elizabeth came in, the smile turned into a beam and Brenda beckoned her over.

"It's good news, Elizabeth. Robin's brother has been telling me . . ."

It was all Elizabeth could do to stop herself bursting out laughing. She couldn't wait to hear the story Robin had spun.

". . . all about the accident. I've agreed that he can take you to the hospital now to see Robin, but you must promise to be back in an hour or so, because the other girls will have to cover for you."

Elizabeth found herself being ushered towards the door by Robin.

"Thank you Miss . . . er . . . Brenda. It's ever so kind of you."

"Oh, think nothing of it. Off you go with Sebastian, and just get back as quickly as you can."

Outside, the traffic warden had finished her paperwork and was sealing it in the polythene bag. Robin took it from her with a grin.

"Save the ratepayers a bit of sticky tape, eh?"

The warden was relieved by the lack of aggression and did her best to smile. It nearly worked. In the car, Elizabeth was convulsed with laughter.

"Sebastian? Sebastian? Who's Sebastian? And how on earth did you turn Battling Brenda into a human being?"

Robin switched on the engine, checked his rear-view mirror and pulled sharply out into the line of traffic.

"Where are we going, Robin? This is ridiculous. I've got a job to do."

Robin grinned as he accelerated to overtake several cars in the middle of the road.

"Fear not, young maiden. The gallant Sebastian has charmed the dragon and you are free to fly away with me in my red super-charger."

Elizabeth's giggles subsided as they sped up the main street at an alarming speed.

"Come on, Robin. Who's Sebastian and what did you say to the dragon, for goodness sake? I told her you were lying in hospital desperately ill."

The car slowed to about fifty as they took a sharp left-hand bend, and headed out towards Ambridge.

"It's all right. I was intercepted by one of your friends as I went into the office and she told me the tale you had spun to the delightful Miss Morgan."

"That must have been Jenny Hinds. I thought Brenda Morgan would soon spread the story round the office."

"Nice one, Elizabeth. Got you a lot of sympathy, and it gave me the perfect opportunity to play the white knight. I said I was your lover's brother, Sebastian, and that he had sent me to bring you to his hospital bedside, where it was touch and go as to whether he'd live."

Elizabeth forgot her crossness of the morning and the night before. That was the charm of Robin. He could get away with almost anything.

"So, unless your speeding actually does land us both in hospital, where are we going?"

"Nowhere in particular. I wanted to give you the flowers by way of an apology for last night. You clearly can't take them back to your office so I thought we'd nip over to Brookfield and put them in some water right away."

"You're absolutely mad, Robin Fairbrother."

"Maybe that's why you like me so much."

"Who says I like you?"

"I do . . . almost as much as I like you."

Elizabeth giggled and put her hand on top of Robin's, as he changed gears. She might even have kissed him, if the passenger seat hadn't been so far away from the driver's seat. The car came to a halt in a very quiet lane just the other side of Lakey Hill from Brookfield. Robin switched off the engine, got out and walked round to her side. He opened the door and bent in towards her. She knew he was going to kiss her and closed her eyes in anticipation of a melting embrace . . . until she suddenly realised that wasn't what she wanted at all.

"Not so fast, Mr Fairbrother. You can't sweep me off my feet with a bunch of flowers. It takes more than that to make up for leaving me standing in the pouring rain, and then sitting for a whole evening drinking Algerian wine and listening to Nelson Gabriel's life story."

Robin drew back.

"I am sorry about last night. I tried to explain on the telephone, but you wouldn't give me a chance."

Elizabeth looked up at him.

"Look, Robin, I don't need any explanations. If you're like the average man, they'll all be half-lies anyway. So please don't insult my intelligence with explanations: the apology is fine. It was very sweet of you to come to the office . . . although I could have done without the crazy story to Brenda Morgan! Thank you for the flowers – they're very beautiful. Now if you'll drive me home I'll put them in water and then I have to get back to work."

Suitably chastened, Robin got back in and re-started the car. On the short drive to Brookfield he made no attempt to deny her comments about half-lies, nor did he try to follow her into the farmhouse when they arrived. Elizabeth was relieved that there was no one in. She didn't want to have to explain about the flowers to her parents, who would only worry even more about her relationship with Robin. She filled a vase with water, took it upstairs to her bedroom and spent a few minutes arranging the flowers. Looking at them, she realised how confused she was. One of the things she liked about Robin was that in all the time they'd known each other he had never once pressed her on anything or overstepped the mark. At the same time, she sometimes felt it would be quite nice if he were a little more forceful. It might be fun if he overwhelmed her with passion once in a while. She wondered how different it would be if he was divorced. According to her girlfriends, that was never likely to happen. They said if he was going to divorce his wife he would have done it long ago, and she feared they might be right.

On the way back to Borchester, Robin drove almost sedately and said little. His high spirits seemed to have evaporated and he looked rather crestfallen. It was the silence that made Elizabeth realise they had entered a new phase of their relationship. It was friendship and not romance, and she wasn't sure whether or not to be sad. Was she gaining or losing? She didn't know . . . and probably wouldn't until it was too late to do anything about it either way.

As she was getting out of the car at the *Echo* office, she remembered Jack Woolley's message.

"By the way, Robin, if you get a garbled message from your secretary, it was from me. Jack Woolley would like you to give him a ring to discuss your wine prices. I think there could be some good business in it but I warn you now, he's looking for a decent discount."

Robin nodded his head sadly.

"Thanks, Elizabeth. That's the story of my life. Business is always good but it doesn't seem to leave much room for other things."

CHAPTER FOUR

When Helen Stevenson arrived for supper at Brookfield the next evening, she was surprised to find herself
in the middle of an Archer family occasion. Elizabeth
hadn't mentioned that they'd be sharing the meal with
her parents, brother, sister, brother-in-law, two aunts
and an uncle. Any initial guilt Helen may have felt
about intruding was quickly swept away, and she was
made to feel at home by Elizabeth's parents, Phil and
Jill. The Archers were known for their hospitality and
they were obviously delighted that their daughter had
brought a female friend home for a change.

Phil, described as being in his dotage by Elizabeth,
was clearly taken by Helen's mature good looks and
was particularly charming in his olde worlde way. If
he'd been only slightly more attentive Elizabeth would
have said he was fussing, but Helen didn't seem to
mind. Jill, despite being in and out of the kitchen, kept
up a lively long-distance conversation.

The others at the supper table were Elizabeth's
brother David, who worked on the farm with his
father; her married sister Shula, who was a land agent;
Shula's husband Mark Hebden, a solicitor; her aunt
Christine, who bred and trained horses; Christine's
husband George Barford, the local gamekeeper; and
her aunt Peggy Archer, who helped out part-time in the
same office as Shula.

No one told Helen what the occasion was, but she
worked out that it was probably an advance celebration
of George and Christine's ninth wedding anniversary.
She also got the impression that the Archer family
didn't need much of an excuse for a get-together. For
most people it would have been an intimidating
experience, but Helen had the easy confidence of a
good journalist and she was soon involved in several
conversations. Elizabeth sat back and watched in
admiration. She also pricked up her ears on various

occasions when she heard titbits of family gossip she hadn't heard before.

What amazed her most was that her parents started talking about their courting days and how they first met. They were always reminiscing, but she hadn't heard them go back that far before. All she knew was that they'd met at the local fete some time in the Dark Ages. One of her dad's favourite lines was "as fete would have it". She'd heard it a million times and she prayed he wouldn't embarrass her by using it this evening. Thankfully, he didn't.

"Do you remember what you were wearing that day at the village fete, Jill?"

Jill blushed.

"What I was wearing? Don't be daft, Phil. It was more than thirty years ago."

It was clear that Phil *could* remember, so while Jill tried to change the conversation, Elizabeth egged him on.

"Go on, Dad. Tell us what it was."

"I remember it so well, Jill. You were wearing a yellow dress and your hair was very blonde. It was cut really short. You looked gorgeous. I first saw you through the viewfinder of my cine-camera, and I think I fell in love with you on the spot."

Jill had stopped blushing and was looking mischievous.

"You're beginning to sound like Maurice Chevalier! It's funny, though. I've never told you before, but the only reason I was at the fete was because I had a crush on Humphrey Lyttelton."

Phil laughed.

"Oh, did you now? And how does he come into the story?"

"What? With your memory of that special day, you can't remember who opened the fete?"

"Good lord, yes. It was Humph. I remember now. That's why I was taking so many shots. I was making a film for the local cine club."

To the family's horror, Helen Stevenson asked the inevitable question.

"Do you still have the film?"

Family photographs and films were always being trotted out by the Archers, and everyone around the table – apart from Helen – gave great sighs of relief when Jill quickly said it had been lost. Helen looked disappointed.

"What a shame. It would have made a nice item for our diary column if you'd actually captured your very first moment of meeting on film. It would have been a lovely story."

Elizabeth looked at Helen in frustration. She hadn't seen the potential of the anecdote, and it made her realise that a journalist had to be on duty all the time. You never knew when you might pick up a newsworthy item. While she was writing headlines in her mind, her sister Shula was only interested in the gossip. She wanted to know more about their parents' early romance.

"Tell us about how you proposed, Dad. I bet that was really romantic."

Phil shook his head.

"Well it was and it wasn't. It was, if you think sending a telegram pleading with a girl to come back to you as soon as possible is romantic, but not if you find large railway stations rather soul-destroying places. Jill was working somewhere – I've forgotten where. Anyway, I wired her to meet me at New Street Station in Birmingham, and that's where I popped the question."

Elizabeth looked dismayed.

"Oh Dad. Not on a station platform? That's really boring. You weren't on the right lines at all!"

Everyone laughed and Christine took over the conversation.

"If you think that's boring you should hear about the way George proposed to me."

Elizabeth heaved a noisy sigh.

"Oh no, Auntie Chris, not another ancient love story."

"What do you mean 'ancient'? I'll have you know that the good Mr Barford and I have only been married for

nine years coming up. Even a child like you can't
think that nine years is all that long ago."

"I'm not a child!"

Elizabeth looked as if she was going to get cross,
but George Barford intervened.

"Come on, you two, no squabbling in front of
guests. Nobody wants to hear about our domestic
affairs. It's beginning to sound like one of those soap
operas on television . . . *Dynasty* or *The Colbys* . . .
maybe we could call this one *The Archers*. It could run
for years."

Helen was the only one who didn't laugh.

"Please do go on, Mr Barford. You say it sounds
like a soap opera. Well, to an outsider it's every bit as
fascinating. I'd love to hear about how you all met and
proposed."

She nearly mentioned again that it could make a
very interesting feature for the *Echo*, but realised that
on this occasion, discretion was definitely the better
part of valour.

George shook his head.

"No, lass, that kind of yarn's not for me. It's our
Chris who has the photographic memory. You'd
better ask her about it."

Christine couldn't tell whether George was just
being his dour Yorkshire self or genuinely didn't want
to be publicly reminded about the circumstances of
their getting together. They had both been married
before. Christine's husband, Paul Johnson, had left
her after getting into financial difficulties, and had
then been killed in a car accident in Germany not long
afterwards. George had left his wife in Yorkshire and
come to Ambridge to work while the divorce was
being arranged. Christine felt no one would want to
hear all that again, but she didn't know where to start.
She looked unsure of herself.

Elizabeth came to her rescue. She could tell Helen
was genuinely interested, and she suspected there was
material here for an article of some sort.

"Oh, please go on Auntie Chris. Don't take any notice of me. I was only teasing."

"I know you were teasing, Elizabeth, but it does sound a bit like a history lesson now. Let's change the subject."

She might have got away with it if Phil hadn't been the host. Mark and Shula were definitely on her side, presumably because they knew it would be their turn next. David was clearly bored with the topic and Peggy Archer looked wistful. She'd been a widow for more than fifteen years, and certainly wouldn't want to be reminded of her courting days. Phil, however, was adamant.

"Come on, sis, you can't disappoint our guest."

Christine shrugged.

"Oh, all right, but it's not in the least romantic, I warn you. After we'd known each other a while, I remember George going back to Yorkshire for a few days. The few days turned into a fortnight, and then when he came back – unlike my gallant brother – he said he didn't like my new hairstyle on which I'd spent a small fortune. And that was after I'd gone to the trouble of borrowing a car to meet him at the station."

Elizabeth let out another sigh of dismay.

"Oh, no. Not another platform proposal?"

George smiled.

"No fear. We Yorkshiremen are much too cautious to do owt on the spur of the moment. It was two days later when I asked her if she wanted to be wed."

Everyone turned to look at Christine as she burst out laughing.

"Cautious? Is that what you call it? You asked me to marry you, and then wouldn't let me give you an answer. I had to pursue you for nearly a week before you would let me say 'yes', which I would have done on the spot."

Phil shifted uncomfortably in his chair, but said nothing. He felt guilty because he had been against the marriage initially and had tried to warn his sister off the

Yorkshireman. Most people had known about George's drink problem, and Phil had seen what alcohol had done to his elder brother Jack – it had eventually killed him and left Peggy a widow with three children to bring up. He guessed George had known about the family's disapproval, and that was why he had given Christine so much time to make up her mind. But it had all worked out for the best. In any case, only Jill knew that side of the story and like the tactful wife she was, she said nothing. Everyone else laughed.

Shula looked at her watch, but it was much too early to leave. She resigned herself to recalling her on-again off-again engagement to Mark. Mark wore his serious I'm-a-solicitor look and promised to be of no help in the ordeal, so she decided to leap in at the deep end.

"I think the first time Mark proposed was very romantic. It was on a New Year's Eve. We'd had a furious row over something to do with blood sports. It'd been going on for days, and I thought it was going to be the end of a wonderful romance. Then, at this party, he managed to drink enough champagne to realise there was more to life than matters of principle, and out popped the question."

Helen looked puzzled.

"You said the 'first time'. Was there another proposal?"

Shula looked across at Elizabeth with raised eyebrows.

"What? Do you mean my little sister hasn't filled you in on how I jilted poor Mark at the last minute, and sent him rushing into the arms of another woman . . . the barmaid at a certain Borchester wine bar to be precise. Congratulations little sister. When did you take your vow of silence?"

Elizabeth protested, but feebly. Her reputation as a gossip was too great to deny.

"Don't be beastly, Shula. Anyway I only relay fascinating pieces of gossip. Not boring old-hat stuff like you and Mark doing the parting-is-such-sweet-sorrow routine."

For a moment Helen looked quite exasperated at the interruption, but she recovered quickly.

"So how did you and Mark get together again, Shula?"

"Oh, that wasn't romantic at all. I had to call on his services as a solicitor to defend me on a motoring offence."

This time Mark interrupted.

"It wasn't a motoring offence. The charge was 'taking and driving away a motor vehicle without the owner's permission' and that's an indictable offence for which you could have gone to prison for six months. You were jolly lucky to have such a good solicitor to defend you."

Helen was slightly shocked.

"But taking and driving away a car means stealing it, doesn't it?"

Mark became almost pompous.

"No, it doesn't. You should know better than that if you're a journalist. In theft there has to be an intent to deprive the owner permanently of the article in question . . ."

Shula stopped him in full flight.

"No lectures this evening, Mark, please."

"But I was only trying . . ."

"I know what you were trying to do . . ."

"I didn't want Helen to get the wrong idea about the offence you committed, that's all."

Elizabeth giggled.

"Come on, sis, own up. Tell Helen about how you ended up in the clink after a riotous night on the town with Nigel."

Mark got slightly huffy at the mention of his former rival. Nigel Pargetter was one of the Borsetshire county set and a bit of a Hooray Henry. His family lived in one of the neighbouring villages, but before he had started working in London, he had spent most of his time in

Ambridge. His major crime, however, was that he'd stepped in to woo Shula while Mark had been off the scene. More recently, Elizabeth had become the focus of Nigel's amorous attentions during his regular trips from the City, but Mark had a long memory and was unlikely to forgive him in a hurry.

"The whole thing was Pargetter's fault. He got drunk at a dance and couldn't find his car when it was time to go home."

Shula and Elizabeth laughed in unison as they remembered the incident. When she'd got over the trauma of being arrested, Shula had given Elizabeth a demonstration of Nigel's drunken walk and slurred speech as he tried to charm the policeman who was threatening to throw them into gaol. Mark was not amused.

"As I was saying . . . when Pargetter couldn't find his own car and saw a friend's car with the keys in the ignition, he decided to borrow it. Shula had the good sense not to let him drive, but just as she got into the driving seat they were apprehended by the local police. It wasn't his friend's car at all. That silly blighter, Pargetter, being as drunk as a lord, couldn't explain things and they both ended up in the cells."

Shula had stopped laughing and was starting to get uncomfortable.

"Please, Mark, we've had enough of all that now. I'm sure Helen's not interested in Nigel."

She carried on nervously, not waiting for Helen's reaction.

"We were talking about proposals, weren't we? Mark got me off the charges all right, but then he ran away to Hong Kong so I couldn't get my hands on him. It took a year for him to see the light, and when he came back he proposed – wait for it – at Birmingham airport!"

Elizabeth looked at Helen apologetically

"I'm sorry, Helen. I think the scriptwriters have been on this particular soap opera too long. There's far too much repetition."

Jill interrupted.

"That's very rude, Elizabeth, and anyway we haven't heard Peggy's story yet. You just sit there and be quiet for a bit."

Elizabeth blushed. She hated being treated like a child, and being scolded in front of Helen Stevenson was doubly irritating. Although Helen was nearly twice her age, she had a sparkle and vitality that took all the fear out of being forty. She never seemed old, and Elizabeth was delighted that they seemed to be becoming friends despite the age gap. She so wanted to appear grown up, and being told off by her mother didn't help. She wanted to protest that she was nearly twenty-one, but when she saw Helen smiling at her she realised it wasn't necessary. Helen understood. So did Peggy Archer.

"It's all right, Jill. My story won't take long, and before anyone else says it, I'll admit that it really is ancient history. I met Jack more than forty years ago in the middle of the Second World War. He was in the army and I was in the ATS – and for your information, young Elizabeth, that was the prehistoric forerunner of the Women's Royal Army Corps! We both ended up in the same depot. Hitler proved to be every bit as effective as Cupid in those days, and Jack proposed in the middle of an air-raid alarm. I accepted, and we had a special licence to be married within three days. Crash, bang, wallop you might say."

They all laughed appreciatively at her brevity. No one pressed her for further details, and Jill took the opportunity to break up the conversation by suggesting they all went into the sitting room for coffee. As they went through, Elizabeth steered Helen to the two chairs furthest from the big inglenook fireplace.

"I'm sorry about all this, Helen. You must find it terribly boring. When we've had coffee, perhaps we could slip off to the local pub and get away from the Archer clan."

"Don't be sorry. It's lovely to be welcomed into such a big family. I miss it a lot. My family are all down in the

West Country so I don't see much of them. I visit my mother, of course, but she's getting on a bit and doesn't entertain very often. If I want to see my brother and sisters I have to trek over to them, and then James gets fed up."

"What about his family?"

"They're up in the north-east, and that could hardly be further away. We get up there as often as we can, but again it means a great round trip if we want to see them all. We never get the chance to sit down with everyone together like this. You're very lucky."

David came across and sat beside them.

"I'm sorry I didn't take much part in the conversation over dinner, but as a mere bachelor I didn't feel I had much to offer on that particular topic."

Elizabeth winced. David, she feared, was going to make an ass of himself by trying to chat up Helen. But Helen was more than ready to deal with that.

"So, on what particular topic do you feel you have something to offer?"

David was equally quick in reading the warning signals.

"Oh, I haven't got anything to say at all about me. I just wanted to hear something about journalism. Elizabeth here has been rabbiting on about it for months now, and I wondered what its fatal fascination was?"

Elizabeth could almost see Helen climb on to her soapbox.

"Well, it's probably because it's much more than a job. It's a way of life, I suppose. There's no nine-to-five routine. You're always on duty because you never know when you're going to stumble on your next story."

David was in an argumentative mood.

"You mean if something had come up in this evening's conversation you would have rushed off to make a newspaper story out of it? Isn't that a bit parasitic?"

Helen was unabashed.

"Most of us are parasites in one way or another. We all live off each other. But the answer to your first question is 'no'. I wouldn't write stories about private conversations. What usually happens is that something somebody says triggers off an idea and I'll go off and work out a feature from there. There's nothing wrong with that, is there?"

"Well, it depends . . ."

"On what?"

"On whether or not the person concerned knows what you're up to. I mean, it's not very nice to sit pumping people half the evening so you can get a story out of them. Isn't that invasion of privacy or something?"

Elizabeth listened with interest. She was out of her depth, but delighted that Helen was more than holding her own.

"I hope you're not suggesting I've come here this evening in search of a story. I haven't. I've simply been enjoying a very pleasant social occasion. If something had come up that I wanted to write about I'd have said so, and the individuals concerned could then have made up their minds about whether or not to co-operate. Anyway, invasion of privacy usually means something else, and I don't think you're likely to find someone on a paper like the *Borchester Echo* committing that offence."

"Why not? Aren't all journalists the same when it comes down to it?"

Helen looked scornful.

"Are all farmers the same? Do you all spend your time trying to fiddle quota payments and grants? Do you all drive around in flashy cars pleading poverty? Of course all journalists aren't the same. There's a big difference between Fleet Street and a small community paper like ours."

David tried to interrupt but Helen swept on without pausing for breath.

"I was trained on a little one-man-and-a-dog paper in Somerset. The editor was a wonderful old character called Nobby Clarke, and he drummed the basics of good reporting into me. I soon learned that you were very quickly taken to task if you weren't honest and accurate. You'd have to wait a long time before you got anything else out of the victim, I can tell you. Journalists are a bit like farmers in one way. We're both natural scapegoats. The public like to put the blame on somebody. Food prices go up and it's your fault. Crimes go up and it's the papers that are to blame."

David was determined to make his point.

"Let's go back to invasion of privacy. I notice you skated over that very quickly. Don't you think it's wrong to pry into people's private lives, and make great scandals out of them?"

For Elizabeth it was a bit like watching a tennis match as the argument raced from one side to the other and back again. It was Helen's turn at the net.

"To use your phrase . . . it all depends: it all depends on whose private life we're talking about. I'm not sure that I'd accept the word pry, but I think it's perfectly legitimate for us to take a special interest in what public figures get up to. It's all part of the democratic process."

"What on earth has a politician's sex life got to do with democracy?"

David might as well not have spoken – Helen was too wound up to notice his question.

"Politicians put themselves up for election so they can be different from the common herd. I honestly believe most of them start out with the right motive – wanting to get into a position where they can do something for their community or society or whatever. But they set themselves above the rest of us, and as long as they behave in the way society expects, they'll get the rewards they deserve. The trouble is, some of them aren't prepared to pay the price. They start thinking they really are different, and don't need to stay within the constraints accepted by the rest of us. If there wasn't a strong press to challenge that attitude, it wouldn't be long before we accepted that there was one law for them and another law for us."

Helen suddenly became aware that nobody else in the room was speaking. They were all listening intently . . . to her. She was embarrassed.

"I'm sorry. I didn't mean to go on so much. I'm afraid David got me on one of my hobbyhorses, and I rather rode off at full pelt."

Phil, gallant as ever, determined to put her at ease.

"Good heavens, don't worry about getting a little excited in this house. With all the different political shades among this lot, we seem to spend half our lives debating the pros and cons of the Common Market or comprehensive education or something or other. This isn't what you'd call a passive household. It was nice to have a fresh topic for a change. I don't think we've had a go at the press for quite some time!"

Elizabeth looked at the clock. It was too late to go down to the Bull.

"Look Helen, I'm sorry, but it's nearly closing time. We'd never persuade Sid Perks to let us into the Bull. If it's all right with you, we'll have to plot our campaign to make you the agricultural correspondent some other time . . ."

Of all the men in the room, Mark Hebden was the only one who didn't look surprised. It was Phil who recovered quickest and he tried to put his question nonchalantly.

"What's this? Are you planning to specialise in agriculture for the paper?"

Elizabeth looked guiltily at Helen. She hadn't meant anyone to overhear her comment. But Helen was unconcerned.

"Planning is too strong a word, Mr Archer. I can't even say I *hope*; what Elizabeth means is that I would very much *like* to be the agricultural correspondent. There's really very little chance of it happening, and I have to admit after seeing your gut reaction to the idea I can almost understand the editor's reluctance to let a woman loose in such hallowed territory."

Phil started to apologise.

"I'm sorry, Helen, I didn't mean that at all. It's just that with old Arnold Thomas having done it for so long, one assumes it'll always be an old experienced . . ."

Jill interrupted him.

"Don't you let these male chauvinists get you down, Helen. If you want to write about farming you jolly well get on with it. And don't let them tell you it's a male preserve because it isn't. There's hardly a farmer in the country who'd survive without the help he gets from his wife, and apart from that there are a lot of women doing important jobs in their own right. There's that woman who runs one of the biggest independent sheep farms in the country over at Stratford, and there's another one right at the top of the Milk Marketing Board . . ."

Mark Hebden brought the argument nearer home.

"Don't forget Shula. She's taken over from a man as land agent for the local estate . . ."

Jill was still in full flight.

"There's been a girl presenting the *Farming Today* programme on the radio for ages, and she's very good at it, too. You've said so yourself, Phil. I notice there's another woman producing the *On Your Farm* programme that Anthony Parkin did for years. I haven't heard too many complaints about that. Even the great bastion of the farming establishment, the Royal Agricultural Society of England, allows its quarterly news magazine to be produced by an all-woman team."

Phil looked and sounded exasperated.

"Yes, yes, Jill. We get the message, but I'm quite sure Helen knew all that already. She is a journalist you know. Information is her business."

Elizabeth was elated.

"Gosh, thanks Mum. That's terrific ammunition to fire at Mr Woolley! I think we'll have him over a barrel. Especially if you and Shula are prepared to talk to him as well. What do you think, Helen?"

Helen was rather bemused by the rapid turn of events.

"I'm not sure what I think to be perfectly honest. You make it all sound like a blow for women's lib. I'm not exactly a bra-burning campaigner, and I'm no great shakes at waving banners. All I want is the chance to write about one of my favourite subjects and one I happen to think is quite important on a paper like ours. I mean, how helpful can the national agri-press be to local farmers? Don't you need more local information? Wouldn't regular items in the *Echo* be of much more value and interest?"

Phil Archer could do little but nod in agreement. Elizabeth smiled. She could see the dawning of a new era at the *Borchester Echo*. More importantly, she could see herself on the brink of a new career. Lead on Jack Woolley, she thought.

CHAPTER FIVE

Nelson Gabriel was at his usual tasks in the early evening: polishing glasses and generally preparing for the rush he always hoped for, but seldom got. The business was doing quite nicely, but it wasn't exactly the gold mine he'd planned. With one or two exceptions, the *jeunesse dorée* of Borchester had yet to discover the joys of drinking good wines in sophisticated surroundings.

One of the exceptions was Elizabeth Archer. She often dropped in on her way home from the office, and seemed to treat the place as her private club. This evening she'd arrived shortly after six o'clock, and was now sitting alone at the bar sipping a glass of champagne paid for with her own money no less. It was nice to see her in funds – though it was an all too rare occurrence. She was usually dependent on one of a horde of young men, each of whom seemed besotted with her.

Nelson would never have admitted it to anyone, but young Elizabeth was one of his favourite customers. She was very pretty but, more important, she bubbled and sparkled like the finest of his champagnes. She was born to enjoy the good things in life and she looked perfect with a tall fluted glass in her hand. He had been known to pour a percentage of his profits into her glass himself, but then life was never dull when she was around. This evening, though, she looked pensive.

"A penny for them."

Elizabeth was startled.

"What? Oh . . . for my thoughts? I'm sorry, Nelson, I didn't mean to be rude. I was thinking about my shady antique dealer, and trying to work out how I could find out more about him."

Nelson smiled at the subterfuge. She wanted his help, but didn't want to ask for it.

"I see. You're trying to penetrate my criminal mind again – hoping my insight will put you on his trail. I should've known better than to assume you were here simply for the quality of service offered by your humble host."

"Come on, Nelson, be a darling. Surely you must have some ideas. I know you're not a crook, but you were nearly one, and that's a lot closer than anyone else I know. Can't you think what he might be up to? It's very important to me, you know. My career could be at stake."

Elizabeth had put on her most plaintive look. Nelson almost smiled, but he didn't want to upset her this evening. He knew how much she wanted to become a journalist. It wasn't just another one of her fads. She'd been through enough of them for him to recognise the difference. However, he was still in the mood for some amusement.

"Are you absolutely sure I'm the nearest thing to a crook – as you so delicately put it – with whom you're acquainted? I seem to remember that your dear old Uncle Tom Forrest once peered through prison bars from the wrong side."

Tom Forrest was her grandmother's brother and some time in the distant past, when he'd been the Ambridge estate's gamekeeper, he'd once got himself involved in a shooting incident with a local poacher. Everyone knew it was an accident, but when the man turned out to be someone who'd been flirting with Uncle Tom's girlfriend (now Elizabeth's Aunt Prue), the police had arrested him on suspicion of murder. He'd been in gaol for some time before it had all been sorted out and he'd been acquitted.

"Poor old Uncle Tom wouldn't recognise a shady character if he came up and bit him on the nose! He's probably the straightest man in the whole of Borchester."

"I admire your family loyalty, dear girl. No doubt it extends to your beautiful sister who, I seem to recall, has also been incarcerated in the police cells. But what about that young reprobate Pargetter? He's been inside too, and from what I've been reading in the newspapers, it seems to me that anyone who makes money in the City must have a number of unsavoury contacts. Can't he help you?"

Elizabeth's plaintiveness gave way to exasperation.

"Nelson, I know you can help me. Why are you being so difficult? I don't want Nigel's help, thank you very much. He's more scatterbrained than I am. He'd probably ruin everything."

Nelson wasn't being awkward. He'd already sounded out most of his contacts. None of them had come across Alan Foster or Brendan Cahill. Neither of them had been seen at any local sales, and none of the dealers were aware of any undue competition in buying around the district. So far he'd drawn a complete blank.

"Well, for what it's worth dear girl, I've already put out a few feelers, but sadly to no avail. Your shady customers seem to be extremely shady. I haven't been able to find anyone who's even heard of them."

Elizabeth was excited again.

"Don't you think that proves there's something fishy going on?"

Knowing to his cost that there was a decidedly rough end of the antiques market, Nelson was cautious. And he was determined that Elizabeth should be too.

"Elizabeth, all my enquiries prove is precisely what I've said. Nothing more, nothing less. I admit your two friends sound a little unusual in their methods, but I really would advise you against making any further allegations until you know a great deal more than we do at the moment."

Elizabeth leapt at the use of the "we".

"Nelson, you said 'we'. Does that mean you'll help me?"

"My dear girl, I can hardly sit by and watch you get yourself into some awful tangle with people who might not be inclined to treat you as the delicate flower you are."

Elizabeth leaned across the bar, threw her arms around his neck and kissed him on the cheek . . . at the precise moment that the door opened, and Nigel Pargetter came in.

"Hello, hello, hello. Is this a *grand amour* that I'm not *au fait* with? Have you become a wrinkly-snatcher, Lizzie?"

Nelson carefully wiped the lipstick from his cheek before turning to Nigel with some disdain.

"If that means what I think it means, young Pargetter, I'll thank you to keep your insinuations about my dotage to yourself. I am not a wrinkly, nor is Miss Archer a snatcher of anything. We'd just arranged a little co-operative activity and the young lady was merely expressing her appreciation. There's more to life than sex, you know."

Elizabeth simply giggled and waved her empty glass at Nigel.

"Come on, moneybags, you're just in time to buy me another glass of champagne. Make it a large one if you please, Mr Gabriel."

Nigel looked disappointed.

"But Lizzie, don't I get a welcoming kiss? I haven't seen you for ages and all you do is push an empty champagne glass in my face. Aren't you pleased to see me?"

Elizabeth slipped off the tall stool and leaned towards Nigel, giving him the most sisterly of pecks on the cheek.

"There you are, Nigel. Welcome home. Does that make you feel better?"

She nipped smartly back behind the stool before he could make any further advances.

"What are you doing here, anyway? I didn't know you were in town."

Undeterred by the rebuff, Nigel stretched out to take her hand.

"You know why I'm here. I always come back for the same thing. To see you."

Looking at him holding her hand, it was hard to believe that Nigel was now twenty-eight. He had the same boyish looks as when he'd first turned up at Brookfield more than five years earlier as Shula's latest boyfriend. He'd changed a lot though. Elizabeth remembered thinking of him as a skinny, boring public school boy with all the embarrassing characteristics of a Hooray Henry. Not that it was really his fault – he *was* a public school boy. He'd gone to Rugby just like his father before him, and played at being a soldier in the school's combined cadet force, an experience that had added to his chinlessness. Now, however, he was almost handsome.

"It is nice to see you Nigel. How's the City? Are you still making oodles of money out of the Big Bang?"

When he'd first appeared as a dewy-eyed young man in Ambridge he'd been a very unsuccessful swimming-pool salesman, and he'd gone on to match that lack of success as a brush salesman. Sadly, that was promptly followed by the brush-off from Shula.

"The City's fine, Lizzie, but I miss you."

Nigel had been proclaiming his undying love for Elizabeth for nearly four years . . . ever since he'd realised that Shula was going to marry Mark Hebden. Elizabeth giggled as she remembered the time Nigel had helped her escape from boarding school. She was only seventeen and all hell had broken loose at Brookfield. She'd never seen her father so angry, but then Nigel had never been one of his favourite people. His worst offence had occurred during his pursuit of Shula, when he'd drunkenly climbed into bed with her father one night. Even Nigel had never been able to explain that one away adequately.

When he lost another succession of jobs and his father sent him to do something useful in Zimbabwe he'd asked Elizabeth to go with him. She was glad she'd said "no" because he was back within a couple of months with another failure under his belt. On his return he'd become an ice-cream salesman driving a Mr Snowy van. Elizabeth laughed out loud this time as she remembered how she'd got a similar job as Ms Snowy, and they'd started up a hilarious sales war. At least Elizabeth thought it was hilarious. Nigel didn't because he kept misplacing his van, and waiting outside the school gates when the schools were closed for the holidays. Inevitably he was sacked, and reduced to doing odd jobs around the village. About a year ago, however, he had been packed off again – this time to London, where his Uncle Lindsay found him a job in the City.

Nelson returned with a bottle of champagne and two glasses.

"From my personal experience, Nigel, this young lady is in a persuasive mood this evening. If she's determined to drink champagne, may I recommend a bottle rather than wasting money by buying it a glass at a time?"

Nigel would have responded in exactly the same way a year before. The difference was that now he had plenty of money.

"Oh, yes, certainly Nelson. Do let's have the bottle, and I'll open it myself if it's all right with you."

He took the bottle and slowly turned it while holding on to the cork. There was a slight "sssh" sound, and a tiny trickle of champagne eased out of the bottle.

"*Voilà*, Lizzie! Opened the expert way. I've been practising."

Elizabeth watched as he deftly poured the champagne into the glasses.

"With whom have you been practising may I ask? Anyone I know? Not the titian-haired Sophie Barlow by any chance?"

Nigel was a little too quick with his reply.

"Sophie and I are just good friends."

Elizabeth smiled. She regarded Sophie as one of *her* best friends. They had first met when she had been going out with Elizabeth's brother David, but their friendship had developed from their mutual interest in clothes. Sophie was a design student with a talent for making dresses and skirts and things. She and David had got engaged, and Sophie and Elizabeth had gone into partnership in a little fashion business. Sadly neither arrangement had worked out too well. The partnership ran out of cash and had broken up, Sophie had found a job in London, and she and David drifted apart. The gossip was that Sophie and Nigel had started seeing quite a lot of each other in London. There wasn't any reason why they shouldn't, but she knew Nigel was very sensitive about it because of his friendship with David.

"You still haven't told me what you're doing here, Nigel."

"I told you before – I've come to see you. I got bored with making money, and decided to have a few days off. I made this my first port of call because I guessed it was where I'd find you. And you see I was right, though I must confess I wasn't expecting to find you in the arms of the silver-haired Nelson Gabriel."

Elizabeth gave him a swift dig in the ribs.

"Stop it, Nigel. I wasn't in his arms. He'd just promised to help me with a very important project, and I was giving him a hug as a token of appreciation. That's all. Don't you go spreading any gossip or I'll never forgive you. Nelson and I really are just good friends."

Nigel was taken aback.

"Slow down, old girl. I was only teasing. I didn't think for a minute there was anything going on between you."

He was about to say that he couldn't imagine Elizabeth with a man old enough to be her father or even her grandfather, but he knew she would take that the wrong way because of her relationship with Robin Fairbrother. He moved the conversation on.

"What is this scheme you're hatching, Lizzie? Any room in it for an old chum who's looking for a worthwhile role in life?"

Elizabeth laughed.

"Forget the hangdog look, Nigel Pargetter. It doesn't work with me, remember. I prefer the forceful type."

Nigel squared his shoulders.

"Then I'm your man, Lizzie. With my army background I'm used to giving orders. I did very well in the old cadets at Rugby, you know. I could have gone into the Grenadier Guards if I hadn't had some pathetic chest complaint that left me the teeniest bit wheezy."

"You in the Grenadiers?"

Elizabeth nearly fell off her stool.

"Come on Nigel, you wouldn't survive in the Girl Guides!"

Nigel started to look hurt, but then remembered her earlier comment about liking forcefulness. He poured another two glasses of champagne. It was the only forceful thing he could think of, offhand.

"Right, Lizzie. No more playing around. Let's have the details of this scheme of yours, and I'll decide whether or not I'll back you."

More out of surprise than anything else, Elizabeth outlined the background to the box numbers story, and her determination to get to the bottom of it. Having listened intently, Nigel looked pleased with himself.

"You know, Lizzie, I think I can actually help. I've got some spare cash at the moment, and I've been looking for somewhere to invest it. I'm bored with the stock market so I might just decide to invest in a few nice antique pieces. How about that? You tell me when your mysterious Mr Foster next advertises under a box number, and I'll reply. It's dead simple."

Nelson reappeared to see if they needed another bottle of champagne and overheard the tail-end of Nigel's remarks.

"Take the word of a near-wrinkly, young Pargetter, there's little in this world that can be described as dead simple . . . always assuming you weren't referring to yourself."

Elizabeth had her eager look and she told Nelson about Nigel's offer. He agreed it was certainly a step forward.

"Right then, Lizzie. It's reward time. Let's have my statutory 'thank you' hug."

Elizabeth happily threw her arms around Nigel and gave him a proper kiss . . . at which point precisely, Robin Fairbrother walked into the bar. Nelson saw him first, and beat a hurried retreat to his tiny storeroom. He had no idea of the current state of play between Elizabeth and Robin, but Robin didn't look too pleased.

"Good evening, Elizabeth. Am I interrupting something?"

Nigel looked flustered. Like Nelson, he really didn't know how things were between them.

Elizabeth wasn't too sure either but she blushed.

"Hello Robin, what are you doing here?"

His reply was lost in a sudden clamour as a group of Borchester's nearest equivalent to yuppies came in, and noisily demanded service. Nigel welcomed the interruption, and asked Nelson for a third glass which he filled and offered to Robin. Robin accepted it with little grace.

"I was saying, Elizabeth, I'd hoped to find you here. I thought we might have a chat, but I see you're otherwise engaged so I'll have a quick drink and be on my way."

Elizabeth thought about being cross. She was always thinking about being cross with Robin, but once more she decided against it. The prospect of getting on to Alan Foster's trail was much too exciting to spoil for the sake of a petty argument.

"Don't you start going all peculiar, Robin. If you want to have a chat, stay and have a chat. That's all Nigel and I have been doing."

"That wasn't what it looked like when I came through the door. There didn't seem to be much chatting going on."

Nigel, who had probably been born looking guilty, guiltily wiped the lipstick from his mouth.

"Lizzie and I were . . . er . . . just sealing a deal, kind of. It wasn't what you think."

Wearily Elizabeth trotted out the whole story yet again . . . Alan Foster . . . antique dealer . . . box numbers . . . sounded shady . . . possible exposé for the *Echo* . . . Nelson helping . . . now Nigel helping.

"Anything else you want to know, Mr Fairbrother?"

Elizabeth's sarcasm found its mark, and Robin had the grace to look sheepish.

"I know it's none of my business. I was only teasing, you know. Anyone would have reacted in the same way if they'd come into a bar and seen two young people in a passionate embrace."

No one believed him, but he was allowed to wriggle off the hook by a forgiving Elizabeth. Nigel was glad not to be involved in any fuss.

"What do you think, Robin? It seems straightforward enough, doesn't it?"

Robin nodded.

"Yes . . . as far as it goes, but what happens when you finally meet this Alan Foster?"

There was a stunned silence. Then Nigel and Elizabeth started to speak at the same time, but Elizabeth was given the floor.

"I hadn't thought that far ahead, Robin, but I suppose I'll confront him . . ."

Nigel followed on excitedly.

"Yes, and tell him you plan to expose him in the newspaper for the villain he is."

Nelson, having temporarily slaked the thirst of his other customers, arrived with another bottle of champagne.

"Yes? No?"

All three nodded, but Robin was first to get out his wallet. Nelson accepted the notes gratefully.

"Forgive me for butting in, but may I be allowed to repeat some wisdom I imparted to Elizabeth earlier? At the moment there's nothing to confront the man with. There's no evidence that he's done anything wrong. You can't go up to him and say, 'I'm Nigel Pargetter and I accuse you of using box numbers in the *Borchester Echo*.' What else has the man done, other than arouse the suspicions of an inexperienced young girl?"

Three blank faces stared back at him, but Elizabeth was determined not to be put off.

"Well, maybe we can't confront him yet, but you admitted yourself that he sounded crooked. Making contact with him is the key. Once we've done that, we've got a better chance of working out what he's up to."

Nelson shook his head.

"Elizabeth, you're beginning to sound like the worst kind of newshound from the gutter press. You're presuming that the man's guilty before you've even met him. It's not as if anyone's complained about his activities. No one's come to the paper and said they've had a raw deal after replying to one of his ads. I agree there does seem to be something worth investigating, but if you're going to be a good journalist you ought to be approaching it all with an open mind. I've told you before, there might be a perfectly reasonable explanation as to why the man uses box numbers. Please, let's not hang him before he's had a fair trial."

Robin reluctantly agreed, Nigel looked uncertain, and Elizabeth was crestfallen. Once again she'd been forced to acknowledge that being a journalist wasn't as easy at it seemed. It didn't reduce her determination, however.

"Yes, I think you're absolutely right, Nelson. If I'm going to be a reporter I want to be a good one. We do have to give the man the benefit of the doubt, but that doesn't mean we shouldn't try to find out a bit more about him, does it?"

Nelson agreed, but still wanted to add another word of advice.

"If Nigel will forgive me for saying so, I'm not sure he's best suited to making the initial contact."

Nigel looked offended.

"Why not? I offered first. Why can't I do it?"

Nelson said nothing, but Elizabeth clearly agreed with him.

"You are liable to get a bit over-excited, Nigel. You could blow the whole thing before we have a chance to investigate it properly. Besides, you're not around

71

Borchester all that often these days. What happens if his next ad appears while you're unavoidably detained in the City? So, anyway, who is it going to be?"

She looked at Nelson and Robin. Neither looked over-enthusiastic, and Nelson said it couldn't be him.

"My connections with the antique trade are much too well known around these parts. Even though we don't know him, Foster is almost bound to know about me. He's hardly likely to try anything funny with an insider. My guess is that whatever he's up to, it's the great unsuspecting public who will be the victims."

Robin shrugged.

"Right, so I've drawn the short straw. What next? We sit tight and wait for the man to place his next ad, and then I reply in the hope of meeting him face to face?"

Everyone agreed. Nelson looked at the second empty champagne bottle. He disappeared and brought back a third.

"I suppose this one ought to be on the house."

He poured four glasses and Nigel raised his.

"Let's drink a toast . . . to Lizzie . . . Miss Elizabeth Archer, reporter-to-be!"

They all laughed, but Elizabeth was secretly thrilled.

"Thanks . . . and I really do mean it. You're all wonderful. I don't know what I'd do without you."

When they'd finished the toast Robin put his glass down on the bar carefully, and looked at Elizabeth with a slightly wicked grin.

"There's just one more thing before the pact is complete. If I have the correct information, Mr Gabriel was welcomed into the plot with a kiss. I saw how Mr Pargetter here plighted his something or other. What about me? What's to be my reward?"

With her determination to be just good friends diminished by too much champagne, Elizabeth leaned across and gave him a kiss which lasted slightly too long and lingered just a bit too much. They both ended up totally confused.

CHAPTER SIX

If Elizabeth felt confused about her feelings for Robin Fairbrother, she was totally bewildered the next day when she complicated her love life even further by making a spur-of-the-moment decision that surprised even her. Maybe shock would have been a better description of her feelings when she realised what she'd done. She'd accepted an invitation to spend the weekend with another of the men in her life. She could hardly believe it . . . but she'd just agreed to go to Berlin to visit Terry Barford!

Terry Barford? Berlin? How on earth was she going to explain it to Robin? Come to that, she'd have to do some fast talking with her parents. Terry, her Aunt Christine's stepson, was serving in the army in West Berlin. Elizabeth had gone out with him once or twice when he'd been home on leave. They had both enjoyed the outings but nothing much had come of it, and that was why she had been so surprised – both by his invitation and by the speed with which she accepted it.

On her way home from work, she had dropped in to say "hello" to her aunt when she suddenly found herself talking to Terry on the telephone. He had rung to speak to his father but George was out and Christine was struggling to keep up a conversation. She always found it difficult to communicate with Terry – partly because he was almost painfully shy, and partly because of the age gap. Neither of them would have acknowledged it, but there was also a significant class barrier between them.

Elizabeth's arrival had been a blessing. Christine had swiftly passed the phone to her niece and sighed with relief at getting off the hook without Terry getting the feeling that she didn't want to speak to him. Now she could hardly believe the outcome.

"Berlin?"

"Yes!"

"For the weekend?"

"Yes!"

"This weekend?"

"Yes!"

"How? I mean why? Well . . . anyway . . . it sounds great fun."

Christine's confusion made Elizabeth realise what was likely to happen when she broke the news at home.

"Will you help me tell Mum and Dad?"

"Er . . . well . . . oh, yes, of course I will."

Christine felt very uncertain about doing anything that might mean getting involved with her brother's family affairs. She remembered how angry she had been when he'd tried to stop her marrying George, and she knew Phil could be notoriously tetchy when it came to discussing his offspring. If she was honest, she wasn't sure how she'd feel if the situation were reversed and someone told her that her daughter was flying off to Berlin for the weekend.

"Don't you think it might be better if you told them yourself, Elizabeth?"

Elizabeth smiled sympathetically. She liked her aunt too much to leave her with a predicament.

"All right . . . don't worry, I'll tell them myself. But I expect you to pick up the pieces if Dad loses his temper again . . ."

"What do you mean?"

Christine was alarmed.

"Phil isn't like that, is he?"

"No, of course not. I'm only teasing. Honestly Aunt Chris, you're getting positively geriatric in your old age!"

"Hey . . . hang on a minute . . . don't pension me off yet!"

Elizabeth laughed.

"Anyway, I'd better go and break the good news that the family can have a nice quiet weekend. Bye."

When she got home, she noticed that her father's car wasn't in the yard. That was a stroke of luck. Now she could leave the tricky explanations to her mother.

Jill Archer tried not to show her own anxiety.

"Your father won't like it one little bit, Elizabeth."

Elizabeth put on her little-girl look.

"Oh, Mum. Don't be a spoilsport. You know Dad will be okay if you say you don't mind."

"But that's just it. I do mind. I don't think it's right for you to waltz in here and suddenly announce that you're going away for the weekend . . . to Berlin . . . with a strange man."

"Terry's not a strange man. He's my cousin."

"Half-cousin . . . and only by marriage. I can assure you, Elizabeth, from where I stand that's strange enough! What on earth have you said to Robin!"

"It's got nothing to do with him!"

"You mean you haven't told him about it yet?"

"No, I haven't told him about it yet . . . and I'm not planning to tell him anything. There's no reason to. There's nothing serious between Robin and I. We're just good friends, as they say in all the best gossip columns."

Jill looked quite relieved.

"Well, I'm pleased to hear that anyway. Phil and I were beginning to worry about him . . ."

Elizabeth saw a light at the end of the tunnel.

"Well, there you are then. That's how to sell it to Dad. Tell him he has no need to worry about Robin Fairbrother any more because I'm going to Berlin to see my cousin . . ."

"Half-cousin!"

". . . all right . . . to see my half-cousin . . ."

"By marriage!"

". . . all right, Mum. To see my half-cousin by marriage."

"He's still not going to like it."

Jill was right.

When Elizabeth heard her father's car, she quickly beat a retreat to her bedroom so that her mother could break the news. A few minutes later, she heard him come upstairs and knock on her door.

"I want to have a word with you, Elizabeth."

"Come in, Dad."

He looked grim as he settled himself on the end of her bed.

"I'm not sure that this weekend in Berlin is a good idea."

Elizabeth put on her little-girl look again, but her father was not impressed.

"It's no use looking at me like that, my girl. It's time you and I had a very serious talk."

"Dad, please spare me the birds and bees routine."

"Stop it, Elizabeth . . . that's not what I want to talk about. Your mother and I are worried about you . . . and all these men you go out with."

"Worried? I'm a big girl now, Dad. I can look after myself."

Philip Archer shook his head wearily. He hadn't wanted to discuss his anxieties with Elizabeth, but Jill had insisted it was only fair to tell her exactly what he felt. The truth was, though, he wasn't sure what he felt.

"I know you're a big girl, Elizabeth . . . and a very beautiful one too . . ."

"Oh, Dad! You've never told me that before."

Phil blushed.

"No . . . maybe not but . . . er . . . now look here, Elizabeth. Stop interrupting me."

"Yes, father!"

"And don't 'yes, father' me either!"

"No, father . . . sorry, Dad."

"What I was trying to say was that your mother and I are worried . . ."

"Oh, Dad. You don't need to worry about me. Honestly, I really can look after myself."

"That's not what bothers us. We're worried about the way you treat some of your boyfriends."

"The way I treat them? Gosh, that's a bit of a turn up for the old father-daughter books! You're worried about me leading the men astray?"

"Well, only in a manner of speaking."

"I hope you're going to explain that remark."

"I will if you'll stop interrupting long enough for me to get more than half a sentence out."

"Right . . . I won't say another word."

Elizabeth's initial amusement was turning to irritation. Her father was beginning to wish he'd never started the conversation.

"Well . . . take Nigel Pargetter. You know he's not one of my favourite people, but you really have been leading him a dance for far too long. It's not fair to him or Sophie."

"Sophie? What's she got to do with it?"

"If you didn't keep Nigel hanging on, he might well go off and settle down with her . . . and please don't interrupt again. You said you'd listen . . . so listen. I think you also treat Robin pretty shabbily. He never seems to know whether he's on his head or his heels . . . ."

Phil paused, waiting for the inevitable interruption. It didn't come.

"Er . . . and now Terry Barford. You can't just drift in and out of someone's life this way. I bet you haven't even written to him since he went back to Berlin and now you're quite casually talking about popping over to spend the weekend with him. What is he going to think?"

Elizabeth still said nothing.

"You remember how Kenton was with Emma Jones. He's never really got over her."

Elizabeth's older brother was in the navy. He hadn't been home for ages because most of his shore leave, up until about eighteen months earlier, had been spent in London with Emma. Then, on the one occasion he'd arrived at her flat unannounced, he'd found her with another man. It had devastated him and now he didn't even like coming back to England. Her father was certainly right about that.

"Servicemen are particularly vulnerable, Elizabeth. It's very difficult for them being so far away from home. They need to be able to trust their girlfriends completely.

Now I know and you know that you don't see Terry as the great love of your life, but what's he going to think when you seem prepared to drop everything and rush over to see him?"

Elizabeth couldn't contain herself any more.

"But that's the whole point, Dad. I've got absolutely nothing arranged for this weekend . . ."

"Yes, but does Terry know that? I bet he doesn't. He'll assume you're going out there because you want to see him. What else would he think?"

Elizabeth was now exasperated.

"He doesn't have to think anything. I told him exactly what the situation was. He said he was feeling a bit fed up and I said I was feeling a bit fed up too, and it was a pity he wasn't coming home on leave so we could be fed up together! He said that was a great idea but then he suddenly remembered something he had to do on Saturday which meant that he couldn't come home. I thought that was the end of that, and hung up. Five minutes later he rang back and asked me if I would go to Berlin to join him. I agreed."

Her father looked at her and shook his head.

"And you just agreed on the spot . . . no stopping to think about anyone else. I bet you haven't a clue about how you're going to get there and where you're going to stay. What about money? You're not expecting me to fork out for a plane ticket, I hope?"

"When do you want me to start responding to this inquisition, Dad?"

"Whenever you like!"

"Right . . . Terry is going to sort out accommodation in Berlin and he's given me the name of a company that does cheap flights for servicemen's families. It's the one his father used that time he had to go out when Terry was in hospital. How am I getting there? That's easy – I catch the plane at Heathrow and Terry will be waiting for me at the other end."

"You haven't mentioned money. Is Terry going to pay?"

78

Elizabeth hesitated.

"No, of course not. You know I wouldn't let him do that. He's only got his army pay and that can't be very much."

"So what were you going to do? I can't imagine you've got any cash at this time of the month."

Ten days before her monthly pittance was due from the *Borchester Echo*, Elizabeth was even more broke than usual. Too many visits to Nelson Gabriel's wine bar had edged her into the red, and only that morning she'd had a polite but firm note from the bank asking her to clear her overdraft at the earliest opportunity. She tried to remember whether or not her father had been around when the bank statement had arrived. She took a chance and assumed he hadn't.

"I was hoping you might lend me a few pounds until my salary comes through, but I can see how unlikely that is so I'll just ask the bank to allow me a bit of credit."

Phil threw back his head and laughed out loud.

"Elizabeth, you're living in cloud-cuckoo-land. There isn't a bank manager in the country who'd be daft enough to give you an overdraft facility. You can't offer any kind of security or guarantee that you'd ever be able to pay it back. You've forgotten how difficult it was even when you wanted it for your fashion business with Sophie. Your mum had to back you, as I remember. I'd like to see your bank manager's face if you went in and calmly told him you needed some of his money to finance your weekend in Berlin. He'd have a fit."

"Ha . . . ha . . . very funny. I'm hardly likely to tell him that, am I? I'd say I needed it to help send my aged parents away for a much-needed break . . ."

Her father smiled.

"You cheeky blighter . . . aged parents, indeed. But, seriously, what are you going to do?"

Elizabeth had long since discovered that honesty was the best policy with her father. She decided to throw herself on his mercy.

"I'm sorry but you're absolutely right, Dad. I am broke and I didn't think about money at all when I was talking to Terry. I suppose I took it for granted that you would bail me out as usual. I'll ask Aunt Christine to tell Terry I made a mistake and can't go to Berlin after all. As I said earlier, it was only a spur-of-the-moment decision and I don't suppose it will bother him if I don't go. I'm sure he'll understand."

Philip Archer looked at his daughter and tried to decide whether or not he was being taken for a ride. The original basis of his objection to the trip was concern for Terry. But now Elizabeth had swung the argument round so that his refusal to lend her money appeared to be the cause of Terry being upset.

"How much do you need?"

"I don't know yet, Dad, but I'll pay you back as soon as my salary comes at the end of the month."

"Yes, of course you will . . . and with interest no doubt! I'll tell you what though – if you mention a word of this to your mother, I'll skin you alive. Understand?"

"Yes, Dad."

The bargain was sealed with a hug and Philip Archer retreated, defeated yet again.

Later, in the kitchen, her mother grinned at her.

"I don't know how you do it, Elizabeth. I wish I could twist your father round my little finger the way you do. When he went up to see you he was threatening all sorts of dire punishments if you refused to see the light, and the next thing I know, he comes back downstairs looking sheepish, saying it's probably best if we let you go to Berlin after all. How much is he lending you?"

They both laughed and Elizabeth put her finger to her lips.

"Sorry, Mum. My lips are sealed. I'd be a more endangered species than the great white whale if I revealed anything!"

A little later, while she was looking at her battered school atlas trying to work out how far Berlin was from Ambridge, Robin rang to ask if she was interested in being his guest at a rather smart dinner over in Worcester . . . on Saturday evening. Elizabeth said she would have loved to have joined him but she just happened to have something else on. She knew her parents could hear her end of the conversation so she was deliberately cool. When Robin tried to find out what she had arranged that couldn't be rearranged, she got annoyed because he was obviously assuming that it was some unimportant event. She put him straight.

"How would you feel if I broke a date with you at short notice?"

She could tell from the sharp intake of breath that Robin had suddenly realised the other engagement could be with another man. She hoped he wouldn't ask her a direct question. But he did.

"Are you going out with someone else, Elizabeth? Is that what it is?"

She still tried to avoid answering directly.

"Actually, Robin, I've got the chance of zipping over to Berlin for the weekend and I've already made all my plans."

"Berlin? Just for the weekend. Who are you going with?"

"I'm not going with anybody. I'm just going to see my cousin."

"I didn't know you had a cousin in Berlin. What's she doing there?"

She was trapped, and with her parents in the background she couldn't tell any fibs . . . especially having said that she didn't care what Robin thought about the trip.

"It's not a she . . . it's a he . . . he's my cousin Terry and he's in the army over there."

"I don't think I've met Terry, have I?"

Robin sounded cross and that irritated Elizabeth, although she tried to hide it.

"Come on, Robin. There are lots of members of the Archer clan you haven't met. It's an enormous family, you know."

"You haven't mentioned him before either."

"There are lots of people I haven't mentioned to you before and anyway, what difference does it make whether or not I've mentioned him?"

"It's just that . . . oh, never mind, Elizabeth. I think I've got the message. I'm sorry to be a pest. Forgive me. I'll see you sometime."

Before Elizabeth could say anything, he'd hung up. She thought about ringing him back but remembering what her father had said about the way she treated men, she simply stood staring at the phone for a few minutes. It rang again.

"Oh Robin, I'm sorry . . ."

It wasn't Robin. It was Nigel Pargetter.

"What's the matter Lizzie? You and the lover having a quarrel? Shall I go away and let you two get together again or should I stay and console you?"

"Oh, it's not important, Nigel. What did you want?"

Elizabeth wasn't in the mood for light-hearted banter, but Nigel didn't notice the warning signals.

"I wanted to make you an offer you can't refuse, Lizzie. I've got two frightfully expensive tickets for absolutely the best show in London . . . I've booked a candlelit dinner for after the theatre and I then propose to drive you slowly and carefully back to Ambridge in time for a champagne breakfast at Grey Gables. What do you say? Bite my hand off if you want."

Elizabeth felt more like biting his head off, but he was saved by her father's lecture. She bit her tongue instead.

"When is this excitement planned for?"

"Oh, didn't I mention that? Saturday night, of course . . . it's the only night I could get the tickets . . . they're like gold dust. We're very lucky to have got them, Lizzie."

"Saturday night? This Saturday night? That's rather short notice, isn't it? What's happened? Has Sophie let you down?"

Nigel let out a wail.

"Please, Lizzie, don't say things like that. The tickets came up and I immediately thought of you. I haven't asked anyone else and I don't want to ask anyone else. It's mean of you even to suggest it."

Elizabeth was feeling mean.

"But why on earth do you suppose I wouldn't already have plans for Saturday night? I'm not a little shrinking violet with nowhere to go and no one to take me out, you know. I'm hardly ever at home, and certainly never on a Saturday night."

"I'm sorry, Lizzie. I know you're usually off somewhere with old Fairbrother, the lucky blighter. But the other evening at Nelson's you seemed to have cooled off a bit and I thought there was just a faint hope that my offer might tempt you. I'm sorry."

"Oh, Nigel, for heaven's sake stop apologising all the time. I'm not off with old Fairbrother, as it happens. Actually I'll be out of the country."

"Out of the country? Where are you going?"

Elizabeth hesitated. She remembered that Nigel had been upset in his impossible, proprietorial way, when she'd been out with Terry the last time.

"I'm going to Berlin to see my cousin, Terry. Mum and Dad want me to go, and Dad's even giving me the money for the air fare. Isn't that good of him?"

Nigel knew he was beaten. He gave in gracefully.

"It sounds terrific fun, Lizzie. I've never been to Berlin myself but it sounds an absolutely fascinating place. Do you think you'll get a chance to go across the Wall to the East?"

Before the conversation was over, Elizabeth had stopped being angry and poor Nigel had offered to drive her to Heathrow on his way back to London. She accepted.

On Friday afternoon when she waved goodbye to Nigel and boarded the plane for West Berlin, Elizabeth felt very nervous. She didn't like flying very much, but even worse, she was no longer sure about the idea of seeing Terry Barford. She felt almost like a teenager on a first date. She had no idea what to expect. As the plane droned on towards Berlin her edginess increased, and any minor anxieties about flying were gradually submerged in her growing panic about seeing Terry at the airport. It slowly dawned on her that she didn't really know him at all. Their mild flirtation, if you could call it that – Elizabeth could only remember one furtive little-more-than-brotherly kiss – had centred around their mutual interest in running. As they'd jogged along, in more ways than one, the conversation had been about track suits, training shoes and the other paraphernalia of the sport.

Elizabeth tried to recall any scrap of information that might help the weekend along. She knew all the family background, of course . . . about his parents splitting up, his unhappiness, and then his inability to settle down either in Yorkshire with his mother or in Ambridge with George and Christine. That didn't add up to knowing much about Terry. She didn't even know what sort of school he'd been to, or when he'd left. Apart from running, she had no idea about his general interests. Whenever his name had come up in conversation with the taciturn George, the only comment had been: "Aye . . . he seems to enjoy army life. Suits him." Such was the stuff of a great weekend, she thought!

In the aisle seat alongside Elizabeth, there was a very smartly dressed middle-aged lady who spoke with only the slightest trace of a German accent. She seemed to sense Elizabeth's twitchiness.

"You don't like flying?"

"Oh, no. It's not that. I mean, it's true I don't like flying very much but that's not what's bothering me."

The older woman smiled.

"Perhaps if we talk it might help . . . before you break your fingernails."

Elizabeth glanced down, and noticed that she was gripping the armrests so tightly that her knuckles had gone white. The woman was holding out her hand and Elizabeth had to release her grip to shake it.

"My name is Tanya . . . Tanya Hirsch. Is this your first trip to West Berlin?"

"Elizabeth Archer . . . and yes, it is my first visit. I've never been to Germany before."

"Ah, my dear girl, don't expect West Berlin to be like Germany. It is a strange city . . . cut off from the heart of the old Berlin by the wretched wall and cut off from the rest of Germany by a ring of communist troops."

Elizabeth looked at the woman. She thought for a moment there were tears in her eyes.

"Do you know the city very well?"

"Know it? I am a Berliner. The scars of the city are my scars."

"Do you live there?"

"No, I only visit these days. I can't stand the feeling of being trapped. I'm only going to visit my mother. She is elderly now and never travels. She has always refused to leave Berlin. Even when Hitler became Chancellor in 1933 and she lost all her possessions, she refused to move. The British bombs could not shift her. Now she just waits to die there."

Elizabeth didn't know what to say. Tanya Hirsch recognised her problem.

"Please . . . don't feel the need to express sympathy. I understand my mother's feelings and I am glad she has the courage of her convictions. It makes up for the disappointment we share over my father. He joined the Nazis and was killed fighting for a cause in which none of us believed."

Elizabeth still didn't know what to say. She wished Helen Stevenson had been with her because she felt sure there was a good newspaper article in Tanya Hirsch. But before she could work out any line of questioning, Tanya changed the subject.

"What takes you to West Berlin?"

"Er . . . I'm going to see a friend . . ."

Elizabeth suddenly decided it was silly to pretend.

". . . a boyfriend!"

Tanya Hirsch instantly became animated.

"How wonderful! How romantic! You must tell this lucky young man to show you our city sights by night and our splendid Grunewald – that's our forest – by day!"

She reeled off a long list of places that were "musts" for any visitor to Berlin. Elizabeth was mesmerised and couldn't take it all in . . . the zoo, Schloss Charlottenburg, Café Kranzler, the Olympic Stadium, the Kaiser Wilhelm Memorial Church, the Reichstag. By the time Tanya had finished, Elizabeth was caught up in the excitement and as the plane lost height for the run into Tegel airport, she knew that she simply had to rush through the barrier and throw herself into Terry's arms. It was the only way to get the weekend off to a proper start!

CHAPTER SEVEN

In the event, it was the geography of Tegel airport that precluded any kind of romantic encounter. Elizabeth's plane was diverted to a different gate and no one had bothered to announce the switch, so when she emerged from the tiny baggage hall into the main airport there was no sign of Terry Barford. As the other, more seasoned, passengers swept past, Elizabeth felt a new panic welling up inside her. Logic told her that Terry would be somewhere around or would at least arrive soon. But logic didn't help. She was alone in a strange country. The only familiar figure – Tanya Hirsch – gave a cheerful wave as she disappeared with a uniformed chauffeur carrying her single Gucci case . . . no doubt towards an enormous Mercedes and her mother.

Elizabeth, with no chauffeur in prospect and her mother thousands of miles away, found a wooden bench and sat down, wondering what to do next. She felt a prickle of tears and tried to hold them back. She must have got the dates muddled up or something. Terry probably wasn't expecting her until next weekend. Even worse, she had no idea how to contact him. She only knew that he was in barracks somewhere in Berlin. She couldn't even remember whether it was in the East or West. All she knew was that he was wherever the Russians weren't. That wouldn't be much use to directory enquiries . . . assuming they could speak English. Without Terry's number, the only thing left to do was ring home and admit to being a fool. No one would be in the least bit surprised.

"Elizabeth!"

She almost wept with relief as she turned to see Terry hurrying towards her. And it was relief, not the thrill of romance, that made her jump up and throw her arms round him.

"Oh, Terry. How wonderful to see you!"

Terry looked delighted and hugged her tightly.

"It's great to see you, Elizabeth."

She felt a pang of guilt – she was giving him the wrong impression – and disentangled herself.

"Gosh, Terry, when you weren't anywhere to be seen, I began to think I'd mixed up the dates and come on the wrong day."

Terry didn't take her comment as an explanation for the hug. He thought he was being admonished for being late.

"I'm sorry, lass. I've been here for ages but I was standing in the wrong place. The information board said your plane was going to arrive at gate three and that's down at the far end of the airport. I've been standing there, thinking you weren't coming."

Elizabeth laughed.

"We're a right pair of chumps, aren't we?"

"Aye . . . but never mind that now. Let's go and get you a drink before we face the drive into the city. If we take it easy for half an hour or so, we should miss the tail end of the rush hour."

It wasn't until they got to the bar that Elizabeth realised Terry was wearing a heavy overcoat and waterproof boots. Looking out of the window, she could see it was snowing quite heavily.

"I wasn't expecting snow. I hope it won't be very cold because I haven't got many warm things with me."

Terry looked at her anxiously.

"It's not exactly warm, love. I did say it'd be below freezing point and that you ought to bring warm gear. Don't you remember?"

If she'd been honest, Elizabeth would have admitted she couldn't remember half of what he'd said on the phone. Nor, to her horror, could she remember much of what she'd said.

Two large gins later, she didn't care.

Terry picked up her bag – not a Gucci – and ushered her towards the car park. There he opened the boot of a very smart car. It was a two-seater

Mercedes and Elizabeth looked at it with a mixture of surprise and pleasure.

"Gosh, Terry, is this yours? They must pay you fantastically well in the army."

"No, it's not mine. I only hired it for the weekend so I could show you around the city. I didn't think you'd appreciate my beaten-up old wreck."

"That's very sweet of you, Terry . . ."

She almost added that she'd have been just as happy in his old banger, but as she would have been lying, she said nothing. Sitting in the car, Terry leant across and Elizabeth was sure he was going to kiss her. She decided not to resist him. But he only tugged the safety belt off its hook.

"You'd better put this on. The roads are a bit slippy with the snow and ice."

Elizabeth wasn't sure whether she felt relieved or disappointed. She had a feeling it was going to be a confusing weekend. Terry started the car and they glided out of the car park into the swirling snow.

"I hope the weather gets a bit better. I've got lots of places to show you in Berlin."

Elizabeth tried to remember some of the places Tanya had mentioned.

"I've got lots of places I'd like to see, too . . . the zoo, the Café something-or-other, the Olympic place and, is it Schloss Charlotte?"

Terry looked slightly crestfallen as he carefully eased the Mercedes through the heavy traffic.

"How do you know so much about Berlin? Have you been here before?"

"Me? No, of course not. I was talking to a Berliner on the plane and I got a whole list of sights I ought to see."

For no good reason, Elizabeth felt the need to add that the Berliner had been female. The information brightened Terry's face.

"Well, it's your weekend, Elizabeth. We'll do whatever you want."

"Oh no, Terry, I don't want it to be like that. I don't want to make decisions of any description. I'm in your hands."

"Good. I've booked us into the Hotel Am Zoo. It's very nice . . . small and friendly but right on the Ku'damm . . . that's the Kurfürstendamm, the main street . . . not far from the zoo!"

Elizabeth's nervousness returned. For some reason she'd assumed that Terry would be staying in his barracks. He wouldn't have done anything silly like booking them into a double room, would he? Oh hell! How was she going to extricate herself from this predicament? What would she say to Robin . . . to Nigel . . . to her father?

The car stopped outside a small hotel where the canopy was covered in snow but parts of the words could still be seen. This was Hotel Am Zoo. Terry double parked alongside another Mercedes and got the luggage out of the boot. He had a case and a shoulder bag of his own and looked like a packhorse as he struggled across the snow-covered pavement. The hotel was small and unprepossessing, but the receptionist was very friendly and spoke excellent English.

"Good evening. My name's Barford. I've got a booking for the weekend."

Elizabeth cringed . . . "a booking". The receptionist smiled and she found herself blushing. She could imagine what the other girl was thinking and she tried desperately not to look like one half of a couple checking into a seedy hotel for a dirty weekend in Brighton.

"You have to register."

"Pardon?"

"You have to fill out a registration form, Elizabeth. Everybody does here."

Elizabeth blushed again. She couldn't bring herself to pretend she was Mrs Barford.

"What do I put down, Terry?"

"Just your name and address, of course."

"But . . . er . . . what name?"

Terry looked at her in bewilderment.

"What name? Oh, I see! You use your own name and address. I only made the booking in my name."

She filled out the card and handed it back to the still smiling receptionist. To Elizabeth's great relief, the girl then pushed two keys across the desk.

"There you are. Room 22 on the first floor for Miss Archer and room 34 on the second floor for you Mr Barford. I hope you both enjoy your stay with us."

Elizabeth blushed again but this time because she felt ashamed of having mis-read the situation. She was awfully glad she hadn't blurted out what she'd been thinking . . . Terry seemed oblivious to her confusion.

"Do you want to settle in – have a bath and things? You'd better ring your parents and let them know you got here in one piece. I'll see you down in the bar in what? About an hour?"

"Yes . . . that'll be lovely. And Terry . . . thank you."

She kissed him on the cheek and went into her room where she flopped on to the narrow bed, feeling exhausted. The room was small but seemed to be well-equipped, and there was a tiny balcony overlooking the main street. Below, she could see people scurrying around in the snow.

When she had managed to work out the instructions for making an international call, she rang Brookfield . . . and was unlucky enough to get David on the phone. He was his usual self and made a few pointed remarks about the bed being comfortable and so on. Her father eventually came on the line and asked for her telephone and room number. He said he would ring back to save her money but she suspected he really wanted to make sure she was in a room of her own. She didn't mind the subterfuge and it was comforting to talk to him and her mother.

In the bar, she found Terry chatting to the Italian barman . . . in Italian. He saw her surprise and explained that he'd learned it at army school . . . after he'd done French and German. Elizabeth again felt guilty. With his slow, Yorkshire accent, she'd assumed he wasn't very bright.

"Dino's booked us a table at a little Italian restaurant not far from here, but you'll still have to wrap up well because it's very cold outside. The snow's stopped but it's freezing cold."

Elizabeth ignored the advice about wrapping up. She was disappointed about going to eat in an Italian restaurant in Berlin.

"Can't we eat German food?"

"Well you can, but we won't get in anywhere decent at this time of night. The Germans tend to have their main meal at lunchtime and all they usually have in the evening is a light supper . . . *Abendbrot* . . . that literally means evening bread . . ."

"All right, Terry, thank you but spare me the language lesson. We'll go to your Italian place!"

Terry looked abashed and Elizabeth wished she hadn't snapped at him. It was going to be a difficult weekend.

When they got to Dino's Italian restaurant, Elizabeth was pleasantly surprised. It was a huge cavern of a place but the atmosphere was noisy and friendly. On a tiny stage hemmed in by tables, a flashing-eyed woman was belting out arias which could only just be heard above the rattle of crockery and the buzz of animated conversation.

Despite having booked for eight o'clock, they were still waiting for a table at quarter to nine. Terry had bought a bottle of Chianti Classico and, perched on high stools at the bar, they matched each other drink for drink. They were both nervous so the wine helped to ease the tension . . . and loosened their tongues. From a desultory exchange about the awful weather and how their various relatives were keeping, the talk meandered on to the safe territory of life in the army and the *Borchester Echo*. Slowly but surely they made progress, and graduated to the subject of personal relationships.

Elizabeth gathered that Terry was footloose and fancy-free but couldn't work out whether or not it was out of choice. She told him she had lots of friends who just happened to be men and dropped Robin and Nigel's names into the conversation. She watched his reaction and again saw a look bordering on dejection. But when she added that she didn't have anyone she regarded as a special boyfriend, she was relieved to see his face light up again. By the time the waiter beckoned to them, Terry was relaxed enough to slip his arm casually round her waist as he guided her to the table.

With the meal, he ordered another bottle of wine and by the time she'd struggled through the cheese and coffee, Elizabeth wasn't sure whether she was tiddly or just dog-tired from the travelling. She stifled a yawn and Terry immediately stood up.

"I think maybe it's time I got you back to bed."

Elizabeth blushed. She wasn't sure what to make of the remark but was saved from having to respond by the waiter fussing around with the bill and her coat. Outside, on the short walk back to the hotel, she thought Terry was going to take her by the hand so she quickly rubbed them together as if because of the cold. Another awkward moment had passed . . . or so she thought.

"It is cold, isn't it?"

Terry put his arm round her and pulled her closer to him.

"Is that better?"

She didn't say anything but he took her weak smile as a sign of agreement.

At the hotel reception, Terry collected both keys and Elizabeth was forced to endure a knowing smile from the night porter as they squeezed into the tiny lift. The doors opened at the second floor and she got out. Her heart sank when Terry followed her.

"I don't know about you Terry, but I'm exhausted. I feel ready to drop."

"Wouldn't you like a nightcap? It'll help you sleep. There's a minibar in your room, you know. We don't even have to go to the bar . . ."

"Er . . . no thanks, Terry. I honestly don't think I could handle another drop. I'm almost asleep on my feet."

"Aye, well . . . I'll wish you goodnight then."

Feeling rather guilty, Elizabeth kissed him on the cheek and hurriedly went into her room, leaving him looking awkward in the corridor. Having quickly removed her make-up and brushed her teeth, she was about to collapse into bed when she saw the "message waiting" light on her telephone. When she rang reception she was told there had been two calls. She was to ring a Mr Nigel and a Mr Brother! Looking at her watch, she remembered it was an hour earlier in England. She rang Robin and he answered the phone immediately.

"Elizabeth, I'm so glad you rang. I'm missing you terribly. I hope you don't mind me ringing. I persuaded your father to give me the name of your hotel and it's taken me hours to get the number from directory enquiries."

"Dad had the number as well. You could have saved yourself a lot of trouble."

"Oh, it wasn't any trouble. I guess you wouldn't have been in much earlier anyway. Have you had a nice evening?"

Should she be cruel or kind?

"I've had a smashing time, thank you. We've been to a terrific Italian restaurant and I'm afraid we both got a bit tiddly on the old vino."

"How's your cousin?"

"Terry? He's great. It's lovely to see him again. If I wasn't so tired, I think we'd be talking the night away catching up on old times."

94

"Have you sent him back to the barracks early, then?"

"Barracks? No, of course not. He's safely tucked up next door."

Robin didn't rise to the bait.

"Incidentally, I'm likely to be in London on Sunday. I could hold on and meet you off the plane if you wanted."

Elizabeth had a quiet giggle. She would never understand men. The worse you treated them, the more they seemed to enjoy it.

"That's ever so kind of you, Robin, but I'm not sure which plane I'm catching yet and, in any case, Nigel has agreed to meet me. I said I'd give him a ring at his London flat when I knew what was happening."

"Sorry . . . I was only trying to be helpful. I don't mean to intrude . . . only . . . oh, never mind."

"What were you going to say, Robin?"

"Just that I thought you and Nigel were only sort of sparring partners, you know."

"We are!"

"Yes . . . well, maybe we can get together for a drink on Monday?"

"That'll be lovely!"

"Good night, Elizabeth. I hope you enjoy the rest of your weekend."

As she hung up, Elizabeth felt confused again. She didn't know how she felt about Robin for more than five minutes at a time . . . but she felt strongly enough not to bother ringing Nigel Pargetter. Ten minutes later, she'd changed her mind. She told herself she shouldn't be thinking about Robin in romantic terms, and rang Nigel's London number. There was no reply. Damn him! He was probably out on the town . . . with Sophie. Why did he bother asking her to call back if he knew he wasn't going to be in? He really was hopeless . . . and thoughtless. She did not sleep well.

At breakfast, Terry was bright and cheerful and there was no hint that he'd been upset or disappointed the previous evening. He was full of plans for the day ahead. The first trip, he said, would be the Grunewald . . . the green wood. The German lesson was never going to end, thought Elizabeth. She looked out of the window and grimaced at the swirling snow. All she needed was a drive through a blizzard to some perishing forest.

But the Grunewald dispelled all her grumpiness. As they drove along in the warmth and cosiness of the Mercedes, she marvelled at all the trees draped in snow that formed intricate patterns on the branches. They passed a horse-drawn sled and lots of children throwing snowballs. It looked like an old-fashioned Christmas card . . . a winter wonderland that reminded her of Ambridge. Almost lost in a reverie, she gradually became aware that Terry was telling her all about the forest. He'd clearly been doing his homework. She wondered if it was for her benefit . . . and then she remembered that he, too, had grown up in the countryside.

"This used to be a really dense forest but with all the bombing during the war, an awful lot of trees were destroyed. Since the war, nearly half of them have been felled and used as fuel. I thought that was very short-sighted of them when I first heard about it, but I've since discovered that the government has had this amazing policy of replacing trees. I bet you couldn't guess how many they've planted over the last twenty years!"

"No, Terry, I couldn't guess. Go on, amaze me!"

He did.

"They've put in eighteen million pine trees . . ."

"Eighteen million?"

"Aye, but that's not all. They've also planted another six million deciduous . . . chestnut, linden, beech, birch and oak. I think that's fantastic. It's a pity the British government doesn't follow their example."

Elizabeth vaguely remembered hearing Helen Stevenson talking about some attempt to encourage farmers to develop farm woodlands with subsidies or grants. She wasn't sure whether it was the British government or something to do with the EEC.

"I don't know the details, but I think one or two people are waking up back home and if I'm right, quite a few farmers are beginning to look at timber as a new crop."

Terry looked at her in surprise.

"I didn't know you took much interest in the countryside?"

"You can't live in a place like Borsetshire and not be interested in the countryside."

"Aye . . . well let's show you a bit more of what Berlin's got to offer in that line . . . and don't forget we're only a few miles from the city centre!"

Terry drove on. Suddenly the forest opened up and they came to the broad expanse of the Havel. It was frozen over, and one or two brave souls were ignoring the freezing temperatures to enjoy some skating.

"In the summer, this place is packed. You can't see it properly because of the snow but over there is Strandbad Wannsee, the biggest beach in Berlin . . ."

"A beach? I didn't know Berlin had any beaches!"

"I don't think many British folk know very much about Berlin."

Elizabeth suspected she was being gently rebuked.

The rest of the day was spent seeing other tourist attractions. Elizabeth wasn't impressed by the famous Olympic Stadium. It looked very much like any other stadium and she thought she was going to freeze to death in the biting wind while Terry went on about Hitler and some black runner called Jesse Owens who won a gold medal in 1936. He said he felt a great sense of history when he looked down on the running track, but it left Elizabeth cold.

It was different when they visited the Reichstag . . . the former parliament building, seat of Hitler's puppet government. She was horrified to see the Nazi banners filling the huge windows, but fascinated when she discovered that the place had been converted into a museum recording the tragedy of the Hitler period.

Behind the Reichstag, Elizabeth got her first close-up look at the Wall. Terry showed her an observation platform where she could climb up to look over into East Berlin. It shocked her to see the Communist guards only a hundred yards away, armed with automatic rifles and watching them through binoculars. On the west side of the Wall, there was a mass of graffiti in various languages expressing the free world's horror of a wall built to keep people *in*, rather than out.

As they stared across into the East and then as they walked alongside the Wall, Terry said very little. He stopped and pointed to a small wooden cross erected on the spot where a young East Berliner had been shot trying to escape. The poignant memorial said the man had been born in a totalitarian state in 1950 and died in freedom . . . though only by six feet . . . in 1971.

When Elizabeth had mentioned the Berlin visit in the *Echo* office, Helen Stevenson had told her she must visit the East . . . to see what life was like on the other side. Elizabeth had had every intention of doing just that but now, as she stood in the eerie silence looking at the cross, she changed her mind. She couldn't understand the ugliness and fear that had driven a young man, only a few months older than her, to brave the machine-guns and the savage dogs for the chance of a better life in the West. She decided she didn't want to understand.

"I think I've gone off Berlin, Terry. Do you mind if we get away from this awful Wall?"

Terry nodded his head and gently led her back to the car.

"I know this is a terrible place, Elizabeth, but I'm not sorry I brought you here. It's only somewhere like this that makes you really understand what freedom is about."

If he was apologising for being a soldier, he needn't have bothered. Elizabeth understood and approved.

The rest of the weekend passed uneventfully. Terry reorganised the sight-seeing plans to avoid places like Checkpoint Charlie and anything else connected with either the war or the cold war. Instead he showed Elizabeth the art galleries, museums and cafés . . . took her for a walk through the zoo and insisted that she viewed the whole city from five hundred feet up the Radio Tower (which he kept calling the *Funkturm*).

On Saturday night, after a lovely meal in a very smart restaurant, he was the perfect gentleman. He walked her to the door of her room, kissed her on the cheek and wished her goodnight. Contrary as ever, Elizabeth would have been much happier with a proper kiss.

The next afternoon, as they waited at the airport for her flight to be called, Elizabeth hugged Terry – enjoying the feeling of his strong arms holding her tightly. She felt confused again. It was becoming too much of a habit.

CHAPTER EIGHT

Two weeks after her Berlin trip, Elizabeth had heard nothing further from Alan Foster or Brendan Cahill and she was beginning to wonder if she was cut out to be an ace reporter after all. She still planned to persuade an unsuspecting Jack Woolley to revive the agricultural correspondent's job, but her attempts to waylay him had come to nothing. The *Borchester Echo* offices were hardly the centre of the universe, and she was getting bored. The thought of taking down tele-ads for the rest of her life made her feel ill, but there were few other prospects on the horizon. She still hadn't come across an eligible millionaire.

The one saving grace was that the formidable Brenda Morgan seemed to have been humanised. Ann Jensen said Brenda had a new boyfriend and Elizabeth agreed it might be true. She'd stopped prying into the other girls' romances – after having gone on endlessly about Terry Barford and the Berlin weekend – and she even allowed them to gossip amongst themselves during the quiet spells.

Elizabeth didn't have much in common with the tele-ad girls, but she tried to get on with them all. The other three lived in Borchester, and she suspected they regarded her as a bit of a country yokel because she lived on a farm. They were pleasant enough on a superficial level, but she couldn't see herself being close friends with any of them. When she had the option, she talked most to Jenny Hinds. Jenny was about four years older than Elizabeth and very sweet. She had an openness about her that even stopped Elizabeth being offended when she made it clear that she disapproved of going out with married men, whether or not they were separated from their wives.

Jenny lived on one of the big council estates with her parents and a brother the same age as Elizabeth. Her father was something on the railways and worked at

Hollerton Junction. Although they weren't very well off, Jenny always looked smart and didn't seem to have too much difficulty keeping up with the latest fashions. When Elizabeth asked her how she managed it, she laughed and produced a credit card.

Because of time as much as anything else, their conversations were usually limited to clothes, the latest records or what had been on television the night before – not that Elizabeth was often at home to watch television. Jenny could never understand what she did to keep herself from getting bored but Elizabeth didn't mention wine bars or the Young Conservatives.

Ann Jensen was the oldest of the girls. She was twenty-eight and had been married for six years. Nobody was quite sure whether she'd also been divorced, but she had a steady stream of boyfriends who seemed to take it in turns to pick her up from the office in the evenings. The other girls found this puzzling because she was so nondescript-looking – with a personality to match. She never had very much to say for herself and the only time she ever seemed animated was when the monthly pay slips arrived and she could see how much extra commission she'd made. She always planned exactly how she was going to spend it, down to the last pound. Although she'd worked with her for nearly a year, Elizabeth didn't know anything about her domestic circumstances or even where she lived except that it was "on the other side of town". No one seemed interested enough to find out more. Elizabeth certainly wasn't. Ann Jensen could stay in her shell as far as she was concerned.

Liz Cole was a much livelier personality, though she seemed younger than twenty-three. Her abiding passion was the charts, and she knew all there was to know about who was where and singing what. She made Elizabeth feel positively ancient . . . not to say ignorant about the pop world. Liz was always humming or tapping out a rhythm. Even when she was typing out the ads, she did it to the beat of whatever hit was going through her head at the time.

There were few visitors to the tele-ads department. Occasionally the classified-advertising manager would call to say how well they were doing or to exhort them to greater efforts if their figures weren't up to scratch. Once in a blue moon, the advertising manager himself would make what amounted to a ceremonial appearance. He seldom spoke to any of the girls, but invariably left Brenda Morgan in a state of nervous collapse. She always assumed the worst, and every time she saw him she expected to be told that her department was no longer cost-effective and was to be shut down. Sometimes she was able to convince even Elizabeth that the end was nigh.

The next office along was occupied, or more often not occupied, by the paper's space salesmen. There were three of them, and their job was to chase all over the county selling advertising space. They were quite a pleasant bunch, as salesmen went, but they were a bit flash for Elizabeth's taste, and she didn't like the way they always complained about the printers' typographical mistakes. Every time an error appeared in print it was company policy to put in a free ad, and that cost the salesmen their commission.

Upstairs was the editorial department, in one huge open-plan office where everyone except the editor worked. Keith Parker had a tiny cubby-hole in the corner where his privacy was protected by a sliding glass partition. In a weak moment he'd once confessed to Helen Stevenson that the most frustrating thing about working at the *Echo* was not having a door to slam when he was angry.

Keith was a nice man. He was about 45 and had come to Borchester after many years working on a big group of newspapers in the Black Country. Everyone said he was a very good journalist and editor, and he was popular with most people on the paper. From Elizabeth's own experience, she knew he was a fair man.

She pestered him endlessly about becoming a reporter, and yet he was always patient and polite. He'd gone out of his way to comment on the few bits and pieces she'd been allowed to tackle, although she still wasn't any closer to becoming a reporter.

Unknown to Elizabeth and the rest of the staff, Keith Parker's preoccupation that morning was about the future of the paper and everyone who worked on it, because an unexpected crisis had arisen. There had always been a natural tension between the editor and the advertising director, with each out to protect his own territory. When Keith Parker had started as editor, there had been an agreed ratio of 60 per cent editorial to 40 per cent advertising. That had been one of his main reasons for taking the job. The ratio ensured that it was a *news*paper, and there weren't too many of them left in the provinces. He'd often agreed to lower the editorial quota when there was a lot of advertising around, and at Christmas he'd even accepted a 50–50 split. Now the advertising people wanted that to become the new standard.

Keith had argued very strongly that editorial should retain the highest percentage, but had said he'd be prepared to accept 55–45. He thought he'd made a reasonable offer which would be acceptable to Arnold Jennings, the advertising director, but he'd just heard that there was now talk of turning the paper into a free sheet. He'd seen what happened to other newspapers when they became free sheets. Ratios had been thrown out of the window, most of the editorial staff had been sacked, and all pretence of being a *news*paper had been abandoned.

So far the scheme for the *Echo* was just a rumour, and he knew it could well have been started by the advertising men as a ploy to weaken his defence against their proposed ratios. What worried him was not being able to get through to the proprietor on the telephone. There was usually something wrong when Jack Woolley avoided him. Keith hadn't talked to any of his staff yet. He didn't like feeding rumours, and he knew that anything he said – short of a total denial – would do just that. He was beginning to understand what old-timers said about the editor's office being the loneliest place in the building.

Outside in the big office, the veteran Campbell Lowrie had some idea of what his boss was going through. He'd just heard the rumours from one of the salesmen with whom he'd been working on a special advertising feature, and seeing the editor's closed door he'd put two and two together. He only hesitated for a few seconds before making up his mind. Age gave him some privileges – and some responsibilities. He heaved himself out of his chair and knocked on the editor's door.

"Can I come in for a moment, Keith?"

Keith, who'd been staring into mid-air, pulled himself together. Campbell sat down.

"Is there any truth in this rumour about us going free?"

The directness of the question didn't surprise Keith Parker. It was one of his features editor's best-known attributes. He decided to be equally straight.

"To be perfectly honest, Campbell, I haven't got a bloody clue. I don't know any more than you do, and I suspect we've got the whisper from the same bloody source. You probably know I've been having a ding-dong with Jennings about the ratio, but I agreed to go down to 55–45 and I thought he'd gone away happy."

Campbell, who resented even having to co-operate with advertisers on the special supplements, allowed his contempt to show.

"Blood-suckers are never happy, Keith. You should know that by now. Once they've got the taste they can't seem to stop. The advertising people aren't interested in newspapers. They're only interested in making money. What does our illustrious proprietor have to say for himself? Or has he suddenly become unavailable for comment in the time-honoured fashion?"

Keith couldn't help smiling. Campbell had been around a long time and there wasn't much he didn't know about human nature.

"He hasn't returned any of my calls. They keep saying he's not in his office and they don't know where he is or when he'll be back."

"That sounds ominous. Caroline Bone usually keeps better tabs on Jack Woolley than that. She knows we don't ring him just to pass the time of day, and she's always been very good at making him call us back."

Keith brightened.

"I've just realised it wasn't Caroline I spoke to. It must have been a temp. Let's try again now."

Keith told his secretary to keep trying the Grey Gables number until she got through. He said he didn't want to speak to anyone but Caroline Bone or Mr Woolley himself. Then he sat staring at the silent phone. The old Scotsman cut through his thoughts.

"Do you want to talk or shall I bugger off and leave you alone?"

He shook his head,

"No, stay Campbell, please. You've been through many crises like this, I expect. What's an editor supposed to do in this situation?"

Campbell shrugged his shoulders.

"I can't help you, lad. An editor's always on his own when it comes to the crunch, but if it's any consolation I've been in lots of sticky positions and lived to tell the tale."

Campbell Lowrie was nearly sixty and had been in newspapers for more than forty years. He'd started as a copy boy on a tiny paper in his native Argyllshire and had worked all over Britian. One of his favourite stories was about the time he worked for the Dundee-based company of D.C. Thomson and Leng. As well as publishing newspapers, they produced the famous comic *The Dandy*, edited by one of Campbell's contemporaries, a journalist called George Thomson. He was the same George Thomson who later became a

Labour MP, a commissioner of the EEC, and was now Lord Thomson, Chairman of the Independent Broadcasting Authority. This final stage in the story was usually accompanied by caustic comments about the banality of television.

Campbell had found his way to Fleet Street and become night news editor on one of the quality papers. It was a tough enough job in itself, but the added stress of anti-social hours and a constant supply of booze had taken its toll. He pulled out just in time to save his marriage and he'd brought his family to the Midlands, where he set up his own news agency in Birmingham.

"Did I ever tell you about my days as my own boss in Birmingham when the wife and I ran the Lowrie News Service from a scruffy old office in Corporation Street . . . in the same building as the old *Gazette* and *Evening Despatch*?"

Keith shook his head, but it wouldn't have made any difference. When Campbell was in the mood for reminiscing nothing could stop him.

"We did very well in the early days when there was a lot of news around and not much competition. There was only one other agency – a good one – run by two brothers. They were very decent blokes, and there were never any hassles with them. In fact they'd often pass jobs on to me if they couldn't cope, especially at weekends when there were lots of football matches to be covered.

"The trouble was, that was about the time when the papers started being run by the accountants, and I suddenly found it harder and harder to get payments out of them. Sometimes we had to wait months after we'd done the work before we got paid. It was the wife who tipped me off about what was happening because she looked after the books. We decided we weren't prepared to subsidise the big boys and we packed it in. That was bloody hard. I'd got used to being my own master."

106

Keith interrupted him as he drew breath.

"There weren't any other staff involved?"

Campbell took the point.

"No, that's true, lad. There was just me and the wife to worry about."

Campbell always referred to his wife as "the wife". In the ten years he'd been at the *Echo*, no one had so far discovered her Christian name.

The telephone rang.

"Hello, Keith Parker here."

He put his hand over the mouthpiece.

"It's Caroline Bone. Hello, Caroline. I'm sorry to bother you, but I've been trying to get hold of Mr Woolley all morning."

At Grey Gables, Caroline had just uncovered a rash of yellow sticky notes, each one asking Mr Woolley to ring Keith Parker urgently.

"I'm awfully sorry, Mr Parker. The temp left your messages on my desk but I'm afraid they got covered up with files and things. Is there anything I can do for you? Mr Woolley's not in this morning. Didn't she tell you that?"

Keith admitted she had.

"To be honest, Caroline, I wasn't sure whether or not he was trying to avoid me. The temp said she didn't know where Mr Woolley was or when he'd be back. That's so unusual in your office that I became a bit suspicious. I do need to talk to him very urgently."

Caroline groaned. She had no idea where Jack Woolley was that morning. He was supposed to be in the office, but when she got back from a quick shopping trip to Borchester he'd gone out without leaving any message about when he'd be back. She was exasperated. She'd tried to drum into him how inefficient and silly it made her look if she couldn't tell people when they could talk to him. She was particularly cross on this occasion because the victim was Keith Parker. She liked him very much, and he never bothered Mr Woolley unless it was important.

"I can assure you, Mr Parker, he's not trying to avoid you. The truth is, the blighter slipped his lead while I wasn't looking, and I'm afraid I haven't the foggiest idea where he is at the moment. If you want to tell me what it's about I'll go and look for him. He's probably walking Captain in the park somewhere."

Keith Parker felt reassured by Caroline's honesty, and he told her about the rumours.

"The problem is that most of the staff – probably all of them by now – have heard the rumour about the *Echo* becoming a free sheet, and you can imagine the concern it's causing. I feel very bad, not being able to tell them anything one way or the other. Do you understand?"

Caroline understood only too well. She was horrified.

"I'm sure you know anything like that would be completely confidential as far as I'm concerned Mr Parker, but if it's any consolation I promise you I haven't heard a word about such an idea. It doesn't sound like Mr Woolley's style. You know how proud he is of the *Echo*. I can't imagine him abandoning the prestige of being a newspaper proprietor to make a few extra pounds out of an advertising sheet. Can you?"

Keith Parker didn't know what to think. He agreed with Caroline's assessment of Mr Woolley, but he also knew that money made otherwise normal people do some very strange things.

"Just ask him to ring me as soon as you can, Caroline, please."

He looked across at Campbell Lowrie's anxious face. What would happen to him if he was made redundant at nearly sixty?

"I'm sorry, but you probably got the gist of all that. Jack Woolley really is out of touch at the moment. Caroline said it didn't sound like his style to settle for profit rather than prestige. I tend to agree with her. What do you think?"

The elderly Scotsman had a sinking feeling in his stomach.

"I wish there were more noble intentions we could attribute to our proprietor. History is full of men who have murdered for money, so I don't think we should discount the profit motive so quickly."

Downstairs, the rumour had just reached the tele-ads department, and a cheerful Brenda Morgan was telling the girls what riches lay in store for them. According to her they were about to inherit the earth. She had a friend who ran the tele-sales for a free sheet in Worcester and the commission to be made was fantastic. Ann Jensen was delighted, and both Liz Cole and Jenny Hinds seemed pleased.

Only Elizabeth was unhappy. She sat quietly at her desk, trying to work out what the change would mean to her. There certainly wouldn't be any point in an advertising free sheet having an agricultural corre- spondent because there wouldn't be enough room for farming reports. Come to that, there wouldn't be space for much else either. She'd seen some of the so-called free newspapers delivered to Brookfield, and the few short articles they contained could have been written by an intelligent monkey. Was this the end of a career that hadn't even begun?

It was almost lunchtime, and because Brenda was in such a good mood Elizabeth asked if she could go off ten minutes early. The response was a cheerful wave, and she darted out before the supervisor could have second thoughts. Upstairs in editorial, the glum faces of Helen and her colleagues confirmed that now was not the time to be pestering for a job.

"Anyone feel like drowning their sorrows?"

Almost instinctively Roy Randall, the news editor, and Alastair Wilson, the reporter, stood up and put on their jackets. Helen Stevenson attempted a smile.

"Let's wait for Campbell. He's in with the editor, but he shouldn't be long."

Almost as she said it, the glass door slid open with a grating noise, and the features editor emerged looking depressed. Behind him, Keith Parker tried to put on a good front.

"Did somebody say something about a drink? Do you mind if I come too?"

Despite wanting to be one of the boys, Keith Parker had always followed the accepted editor's practice of never going to the same pub as his reporters. However, if the *Echo*'s traditions were going to change he'd resolved that this would be the first one to go. As they straggled across the road to the Railway Inn, Elizabeth suggested to Helen that maybe it would be better if she didn't join them. She felt she'd be intruding. Helen nodded in agreement, but Campbell Lowrie caught Elizabeth's arm.

"Come on, young Lizzie, this is no day to be standing on ceremony. You know Jack Woolley better than any of us. Perhaps you can help us fathom out how to deal with him."

Elizabeth started to protest, but the others chorused their agreement with Campbell.

In the pub, Keith Parker insisted on buying the first round. Large Scotches and double gins were ordered. As the drinks arrived, it was Roy Randall who asked the leading question.

"Right, boss, tell us the worst. When do we have to start looking for other jobs?"

Keith Parker looked weary and shook his head.

"The trouble is, Roy, I can't tell you anything. It's still a rumour as far as I know. I haven't been able to talk to Mr Woolley yet. He hasn't been in his office all morning."

Roy was disgruntled.

"Fine bloody proprietor he is – disappears when there's dirty work to be done."

Roy was a thirty-year-old graduate from the School of Journalism at Cardiff University. His left-wing politics didn't endear bosses to him at the best of times, but today he had extra cause to feel sore. He had lost his previous job as television and entertainment editor on a Home Counties newspaper when it had been turned into a free sheet. The company had offered him another job of sorts, but he'd told them what they could do with it.

Young Alastair Wilson sat chewing his nails, and sipped a neat Scotch. He was only twenty-two and the *Echo* was his first paper. He was confident enough to think that, despite the current threat, it wouldn't be his last. He wasn't convinced that producing free newspapers was such a bad idea anyway, and he made the mistake of voicing his opinion.

"Not all free newspapers are rubbish. I've seen a few that do quite a good job of covering local events, and you can't deny that getting them into every house means more people are likely to read them. Surely that's got to be better for journalists in the end. I mean, if the standards aren't good enough the public will protest, and the publishers will have to improve them. They'll only be able to do that by taking on more reporters."

Elizabeth wasn't sure whether to admire Alastair's courage in expressing an obviously unpopular view or cringe at his naivety. Roy Randall was sure of his feelings.

"What a load of . . ."

His outburst was interrupted by the barman who was waving the telephone receiver and beckoning to Campbell Lowrie. As Campbell went off to take the call, Keith Parker came to young Alastair's defence.

"Don't get at him, Roy. He's only a lad, and you never know – he might be right. Maybe when we've looked at our outstanding mortgages we'll all be glad to work for any paper that'll pay us."

Roy was none too happy, but he knew his boss was right. The young lad's comments weren't worth an argument.

"Sorry Alastair, I didn't mean to fly off the handle. As the editor says, you just could be right in the long run."

His apology earned a quick squeeze of the hand from Helen. She recognised the effort it had taken for him to cool down so quickly. She hoped, however, that her gesture of sympathy would not be misinterpreted. She'd had a bit of difficulty with Roy in the past. His wife was a nurse who worked regular late shifts, and Helen had foolishly accepted his invitation to a Chinese meal one night when James was away. The evening had ended with him making a pass at her, and it had taken all her natural charm to get out of a sticky situation without any upset on either side. They'd become good colleagues, and she was anxious not to rock the boat.

Elizabeth was just beginning to think she had made a mistake in coming out with the editorial staff when Keith turned to her.

"Right, young Elizabeth, tell us what you know about the redoubtable Jack Woolley. Is he a two-headed monster who'll sell us down the river or can he resist the pot of gold?"

Elizabeth had been asking herself more or less the same question since she'd first heard the news. She hadn't known what to think when it had been presented to her as a *fait accompli*, but now that it had been reduced to the status of a rumour she felt more confident.

"I can't believe Mr Woolley would do anything to damage the paper. He's so proud of rising from back street boy to wealthy landowner and proprietor of the county's biggest newspaper. He must believe it himself because I've heard him say as much on too many occasions. The only danger is if someone he trusts and respects has been able to convince him of Alastair's argument. In that case, he might do it, thinking it was for the best."

Before anyone could respond, Campbell returned to the table and looked gravely at the editor.

"That was Caroline Bone. She rang me because she didn't know where to find you. She'd managed to track down Jack Woolley, but he says he won't talk to you on the phone. If you want to see him, he'll be available first thing tomorrow morning at Grey Gables. It doesn't sound too hopeful, does it?"

CHAPTER NINE

Jack Woolley wasn't in a good mood. He'd got up later than he'd intended, and had to hurry his breakfast. Captain was barking because he wanted to go for a walk, and it was pouring with rain. He knew he had an appointment with the editor of the *Borchester Echo*, but he wasn't sure what time. He hated being disorganised. That was why he employed Caroline Bone, and she was nowhere to be found.

"Be quiet, Captain. We're not going walkies in that rain. We'll get soaked, and you know that's not good for you. The vet told us that only last week."

Like all devoted pet-owners, Jack Woolley talked to his dog as if he were addressing a recalcitrant child.

"It's no use looking at me like that. I've said 'no' and that's what I mean."

The phone started buzzing in the outer office and he went to answer it. It was dead. He looked at the flashing light on the switchboard, twiddled various switches, and still couldn't hear anyone. Angrily he slammed the receiver down.

"Come on, Captain, I've changed my mind. We will go for a walk. This place is a madhouse."

He had his Barbour and deerstalker hat on when Caroline Bone arrived.

"Wherever are you going Mr Woolley? You haven't forgotten your appointment with Keith Parker! He'll be here in half an hour and you said you wanted a session on the phone with Arnold Jennings before that."

Mr Woolley looked exasperated.

"Well why weren't you here to tell me a bit sooner? I had no idea what I was supposed to be doing this morning. Haven't I got time to take Captain for a little walk? He'll be disappointed."

Caroline put on her coolest voice.

"First of all, Mr Woolley, I wasn't here at nine o'clock on the dot because it was my turn to do the

114

market run to Borchester. Secondly, if you look in both your desk diary and your personal Filofax you'll find Keith Parker's appointment marked in red for quarter to ten. Thirdly, that piece of yellow paper stuck on the front cover of your diary says MUST ring Arnold Jennings BEFORE Keith Parker arrives. As it's now approaching twenty past nine I would personally say that you do not have time to take Captain for a walk."

Jack knew when he was beaten.

"All right, all right, Caroline. There's no need to get over-excited. Can you get me Arnold on the phone and maybe you or one of the staff could give Captain a little walk? He hasn't had any exercise this morning."

Caroline gritted her teeth.

"I am not getting over-excited Mr Woolley. I am simply exasperated. You employ me to run your office efficiently. I work jolly hard at it, and it usually works until you suddenly decide that you're not a hard-headed businessman but a country gentleman with nothing better to do than walk his wretched dog."

"Steady now, Caroline. There's no need to take it out on poor Captain."

"I'm not taking it out on *poor* Captain. It's you I'm complaining about. Do you have any idea what poor Keith Parker and the staff at the *Echo* have been going through since yesterday? Just because you decide to stroll round your country estate without telling anyone or bothering to take the telephone pager with you, dozens of people probably haven't slept a wink all night worrying about their future. Don't you care?"

Nobody else would have dared speak to Jack Woolley in such terms. He might take it from Caroline, but it still made him angry.

"Now look here, Miss Bone, you can't tell Jack Woolley he doesn't care about people. I care an awful lot about all my staff. Don't forget, I started life in very poor circumstances, and I was the victim of bad bosses in my younger days. You don't know what it's like in a small factory where you have to work your fingers to the bone for a few pounds a week, and the boss treats you like a slave. That's how I started when I was a boy. Oh, I care all right. I care very much."

Caroline had heard the story a thousand times, and she recognised the need for a change of tactics.

"I'm sorry, Mr Woolley, but can I please get you Arnold Jennings on the phone? If you don't speak to him soon Keith Parker will be here, and under the circumstances I'm sure you won't want to keep him waiting."

Jack was staring at his gnarled, work-worn hands – hands that would always mark him as different from the old-money country set – and thinking about one particular factory boss he would quite cheerfully have strangled.

"Sorry, what did you say, Caroline?"

The reversion to her Christian name was an indication that hostilities were over.

"I'll just get Arnold Jennings on the phone. You wanted to talk to him about those rumours – about your newspaper becoming a free sheet."

She had chosen her words very carefully, and had put the accent on "your" and "news". It worked.

"Yes I do want to talk to him about that. The very idea of it! Get him as soon as you can, please."

Caroline went out and dialled the direct line to Arnold Jennings' office. When his secretary said Mr Jennings was in conference and had asked not to be disturbed under any circumstances, Caroline's voice turned icy.

"I think you may have misheard me. This is Mr Woolley's office . . . Mr Jack Woolley . . . the proprietor of the *Borchester Echo*. He needs to talk to Mr Jennings urgently. No, this afternoon will not do."

Arnold Jennings obviously had a new secretary who believed that there was no one in the world more important than Mr Jennings.

"No 'maybe later this morning' won't do either. Mr Woolley wants to speak to him immediately. Is there anyone else in the office that I can speak to?"

A man's voice came on the line.

"Look, love, as the girl says: Mr Jennings is too busy to speak to anyone at the moment. Try sometime later this afternoon."

Caroline recognised the oily tones of Jack Englefield, the advertising manager.

"I see, Mr Englefield. Perhaps you would care to explain that to Mr Woolley yourself. Just a moment and I'll put you through."

There was a loud gasp at the other end of the line.

"Just a minute. Who did you say it was? Mr Woolley. Hold on. There's been some misunderstanding here. We have a new secretary. Just a second."

Caroline smiled. She could imagine the flap going on in the other office as Englefield remonstrated with a glamorous but not very bright secretary. There were several clicks and then a loud buzz before she heard the genteel tones of Arnold Jennings.

"Good morning, Miss Bone. I'm sorry if there's been any misunderstanding, but I am frightfully busy this morning and I do have a very important client with me. However, as it's Mr Woolley I will of course take the call."

Caroline was almost inclined to put Mr Woolley through there and then, but she thought better of it. The matter was too important to let pettiness creep in.

"If you don't mind me making a suggestion, Mr Jennings, it might be a good idea to take the call in private. I don't think either you or Mr Woolley would like to have a confidential discussion in front of a client however important."

She threw the switch on the keyboard before he could reply, and spoke to Mr Woolley.

"I've got Mr Jennings now. Do you want me to stay on the line for this?"

When he was having important conversations Caroline was usually expected to listen in and make a note of what was said. It was a ploy he'd learned from a civil servant.

"Yes please, Caroline. I think it could be a sticky one."

She put him through.

"Good morning, Arnold. How are you? Busy? Oh yes, I bet you are. Look here, Arnold, a little bird tells me that there's some gossip about the *Echo* being converted into one of these free sheet advertising things. You wouldn't be up to anything funny, would you?"

At the other end of the line, Jennings smiled to himself. Bad news travels fast.

"All that's happened, Mr Woolley, is that we've had an approach from another group and their initial figures look very attractive."

Jack Woolley sounded as if he was ready to blow a gasket.

"And why wasn't I told about this before it became common gossip among the staff? It's disgraceful. I'm the prorietor of this paper and I have to get my information from the office grapevine. It's not good enough Jennings. I shall call a special board meeting and I'll want a full explanation."

"I'm sorry if there's been any gossip, Mr Woolley. I can only assume that someone saw my contact going into the building and recognised him. I haven't mentioned it to you before now because it's still a very tenuous proposal, and I didn't want to bother you with something that might have turned out to be pure pie in the sky. Now that I know you're interested I'll be happy to make a more detailed study of the proposal. When would you like to call the special board meeting? I could have the figures ready within a couple of days. When shall we say? Friday?"

Caroline marvelled at the smoothness of the man. He had completely outmanoeuvred Mr Woolley, and won a couple of days' grace to perfect his scheme. The betting on the *Borchester Echo* surviving as a newspaper looked pretty poor.

Mr Woolley called Caroline into his office.

"I never did like Arnold Jennings. He's got something up his sleeve and I've played into his hands by giving him another two days to scheme and plot. What am I going to say to Keith Parker now?"

Caroline shook her head in bewilderment.

"I honestly don't know, Mr Woolley. I don't understand it. You're the proprietor – why can't you make your own decision and tell anyone who doesn't like it to go hang?"

"I wish it was as easy as that, Caroline. But you can't give people positions of responsibility if you don't give them the authority to do their jobs. I mean, look at the number of times I've made little suggestions to Keith Parker about what might go into the paper, and what has his response been?"

The phone in the outer office buzzed and Fiona said Mr Parker was in reception. Caroline asked her to show him in, and he arrived, looking very nervous.

"Morning, Caroline."

"Morning, Mr Parker. Mr Woolley's waiting for you. If you'd like to go straight in, I'll get you some coffee."

"Thank you, that would be very nice."

She showed him into Jack Woolley's office and quietly went off to arrange the coffee. Jack greeted him with a cheerful grin and a strong handshake.

"Sit down, Keith. It's a rare pleasure to see you at Grey Gables. Mind you, I'm sure we both wish it was under better circumstances."

"You're certainly right there, Mr Woolley. I haven't had a wink of sleep, and I suspect it's been the same for most of the staff . . . well the editorial people anyway."

Jack tried to sound sympathetic and understanding.

"I'm really sorry about that, and I hope you'll tell them so when you get back to the office. Nasty things rumours. They leave everyone upset and suspicious."

For the first time Keith Parker looked relieved.

"So it is all just rumour? You're not planning to turn the paper into an advertising sheet. I can tell the staff that?"

119

Jack was about to agree when he remembered the special board meeting.

"Well . . . not quite. The directors have got to meet on Friday to discuss . . ."

"But I thought you said it was a rumour? What is there to discuss?"

"Look, Keith, it isn't as simple as you think. It is just rumour at the moment, but a big group has been in touch with Arnold Jennings and they've made some kind of offer. I don't know the details and nor do the other directors. Commonsense demands that we don't just reject the idea without even talking about it. We're going to have to discuss it before we throw it out."

The editor's worried look had returned.

"If you're going to discuss it you must be taking it seriously, and there's got to be a chance that the board will like the idea. It probably means extra money for the company, and without a journalist on the board there won't be anyone to talk about the impact it will have on us as a newspaper. That's not fair."

Jack was getting impatient.

"You don't think I've got the best interests of the paper at heart?"

"I'm sure you have, Mr Woolley, but do you really understand the difference between what we're able to do with reporters and what can be done by the free sheets? My handful of reporters flog themselves to death for the *Echo*. They're proud to work on it because we provide a first-class service for this community. Very little happens that we don't get to hear about. We cover all the local organisations, and we keep an eye on the district council. Can you imagine some of the things that lot would get up to, if they weren't under the constant scrutiny of a lively local newspaper?"

Jack wanted to interrupt, but Keith Parker was in full flow.

"What about all the sports events we cover, and all the weddings and funerals? What do you think would happen to all that if the paper was turned into an advertising rag? I know we get called the 'local rag' at the moment, but that's out of affection. People love the *Echo*, Mr Woolley, because it genuinely tries to reflect the kind of community we live in. An advertising sheet could never do that. The very fact that it's free means half the people never read it, and there are hundreds that never even get delivered."

Jack listened intently as his editor's monologue went on.

"These sort of papers can't support a proper reporting staff. Even our staff isn't really adequate. Helen and the others have been on at me to replace the agricultural correspondent, but I know we can't afford it so I haven't mentioned it to you. In the free sheets, the articles are usually written by enthusiastic amateurs who don't know anything about reporting court cases, libel or anything of that sort. I'm sure lots of them start off with the best intentions, but the pressure from advertising revenue is too great in the end. It always ends in a sell-out to whatever makes the most money."

Jack Woolley was very impressed.

"It's a pity you're not on the board, Keith. We could do with someone who had your commitment."

That was a sore point.

"It's a great pity, Mr Woolley. You know I've always said that a newspaper board without an editor as a member isn't properly balanced. A newspaper's not like other products because it's got a much shorter shelf-life. We don't get the chance to sort out our problems over a long period. Every issue has to satisfy the reader or they simply won't buy the next one."

Mr Woolley had been down this road with the previous two editors, but Keith Parker was different. He had more passion, more soul. Running a weekly newspaper wasn't just a job for him. It was a way of life.

"Look, Keith, I've got your message loud and clear, and I promise you I'm very sympathetic to your point of view. I'd like to give you an answer here and now, but I'm sure you understand why I can't. I'd appreciate it if you could reassure the staff as best you can."

Keith Parker straightened his shoulders and took an envelope from his inside pocket.

"I'm sorry, Mr Woolley, but that isn't good enough for my people. Campbell Lowrie has given the paper ten years' service and he's nearly sixty now. There's no way I'm going to be party to making him redundant. Roy Randall is still only thirty and he's been through this once before. Helen Stevenson has just begun to make her mark after having to rebuild a career because of her husband's travels. Even young Alastair Wilson is so enthusiastic it's not true. I decided last night that if I couldn't get a straight answer out of you this morning I was going to resign. I've already discussed it with my wife, and she's going to support me until I find another job. This is my resignation letter, and you'll see in it that I would like to leave immediately. I don't want to be in on any wake."

Jack was stunned. Keith was the best editor he'd ever had, and more important, he liked him very much as a man. He'd expected him to be angry about the rumour, but he hadn't anticipated this.

"You can't resign, Keith. Don't be hasty. I've been honest with you and told you the whole score. What more can I do?"

"I'm not being hasty, Mr Woolley. I had all day yesterday and all last night to think about my position. In my book, an editor has two responsibilities: one to his readers and the other to his staff. If Arnold Jennings' scheme goes through, I won't be able to fulfil either. But I'm not prepared to stand on the touchline and watch a game I can't take part in. I've never much liked spectator sports. If, as the editor, I don't have any direct influence on the future of the newspaper then it's time for me to quit."

For the proprietor of an influential local paper, Jack Woolley felt surprisingly lacking in influence himself.

"But now it's you who's not being fair, Keith. You're blackmailing me. You're trying to make me pre-empt a board discussion and I can't do that. It's not right. The other directors have got to have their say."

Keith leaned forward and tapped the envelope on the desk.

"You haven't been listening, Mr Woolley. That's my resignation as of now. I'm not the blackmailing type. I'm leaving *before* the discussion takes place. It's not a threat. I'm not putting a gun to your head. I'm just getting out. If you weren't interested in the commercial advantages – and I'm not blaming you for that – you would have been able to tell me categorically that this plan was just a ploy by Arnold Jennings and his boys to make me accept a 50–50 ratio. You can't. Campbell Lowrie was right. There's no smoke without a fire."

He got up to leave, but Jack came round the table and put a hand on his shoulder.

"Please don't go, Keith. We ought to be able to talk this through. We're both on the same side. I know you're very proud of the *Echo* and you regard it as *your* paper. Well, I'm just as proud of it and I regard it as *my* paper too. I'm not going to let any two-bit advertising smoothie change all that. You don't know me well enough. I was brought up in a very hard school and I know every dirty trick in the book. You leave it to me and Mr Jennings won't know what day of the week it is."

Before Keith could reply there was a knock on the door, and Caroline Bone brought in a tray of coffee.

"Do you take it black or with milk, Mr Parker?"

Although she hadn't heard everything, she knew the moment was right for an interruption. Jack was glad of the brief respite, and Keith could only sit down again. As Caroline slowly poured the coffee and generally fussed around, neither man said anything. When she left it was Jack who spoke first.

"Very clever girl, Caroline. She seems to have a sixth sense . . ."

123

Keith was forced to smile.

"Yes, or very good hearing. I'll drink your coffee, Mr Woolley, but it's no use arguing with me any more. I've made up my mind."

Jack pushed his empty coffee cup across the desk.

"You've got me wrong again, Keith. I'm not going to argue with you. You're a man of honour, and if your decision is to resign I've got to respect that. I don't want you to leave, but I'm not going to try to stop you. You might not think it, after what I said about knowing all the dirty tricks, but I'm an honourable man too. I have to talk to my board of directors before I can make a decision. I'm sorry."

Keith stood up again. Jack came round the desk and they shook hands.

"You've been a damn good editor, and I'll miss you. We've had our ups and downs, but we've always been able to resolve our problems. If it's any consolation, you've done more than anyone to make me understand the proper role of the proprietor of a paper like the *Borchester Echo*. I used to think I owned it. You made me realise I'm only its guardian."

"Thanks, Mr Woolley . . . Jack. I hope you remember that on Friday."

As Keith left looking strained and unhappy, Caroline came back into the office.

"What on earth's happened? You look as if you've seen a ghost, Mr Woolley."

Jack walked over to the window and watched as his former editor climbed into his car and drove off.

"He won't be an easy man to replace."

Caroline was stunned.

"What do you mean, 'replace'? You haven't fired Keith Parker, have you? You must be mad. He's the best kind of journalist there is. I've never known anyone with more integrity. He's got the respect of all his staff. They all love him. Why did you do it?"

Jack shook his head sadly.

"No, Caroline, I didn't sack him. He resigned. I agree with you. He's the kind of journalist our paper needs."

"But why did he resign? Why did you let him? The rumours aren't true, are they? You're not going to turn the *Echo* into one of these dreadful giveaway things? What about all the other journalists? Are they all going to lose their jobs? Is money that important to you?"

Caroline was taken aback by her own outburst, but Mr Woolley accepted it without comment. He sat down behind his desk.

"You don't understand, Caroline. I couldn't give Keith the answer he wanted. I'm sure I would have been able to on Friday, but I couldn't today. He resigned on a matter of principle, as he saw it. I couldn't stop him."

Caroline had calmed down a little, and now became practical.

"What are you going to do? Who's going to look after the paper until you can find another editor?"

Jack wasn't in the mood for practicalities.

"The paper will look after itself. Keith had it all tied up very smoothly. Campbell Lowrie will be able to keep things ticking over. That's not what worries me, Caroline. I feel I've let Keith down. I didn't give him a seat on the board because I thought he didn't know enough about business. Well, he might not know a lot about balance sheets and cash flows, but I've learned too late that he knows more about the business of running a good newspaper than I ever will. He's the man I should have been listening to over the years instead of Arnold Jennings."

Caroline poured another coffee and slid it towards her boss. She spoke quietly.

"I'm sorry, Mr Woolley. I spoke out of turn. I realise you're very upset, and having me going off like a locomotive can't have helped. Is there anything you would like me to do? Should I get Mr Lowrie on the phone?"

Jack shook his head.

"Not yet. If I know anything about Keith Parker he'll want to tell his staff what he's done himself. Campbell Lowrie will be on to me soon enough, and so I expect will Roy Randall, Helen Stevenson and the rest of them. Don't be surprised if we also get a call from the NUJ wanting to know what's happening. I'm out to all of them except Campbell, and he won't call before the pubs close at lunchtime."

He pushed his chair back.

"I'm going to take Captain for a walk. I feel more like being a country landowner this morning. I'm not sure when I'll be back."

CHAPTER TEN

Nigel Pargetter was trying to make Elizabeth smile but he wasn't having a great deal of success. Unaware of the crisis in her office, he'd invited her to Nelson's wine bar on her way home, and been very surprised to hear that she wasn't in the mood for champagne but would happily drink as many gins as he cared to put in front of her.

"Come on, Lizzie, tell Nigel what's wrong. You're much too young and pretty to be diving head first into mother's ruin this way."

Ungrateful for both his company and his hospitality, she was at her most truculent.

"For goodness sake, Nigel, you're behaving like a silly adolescent. If you don't stop treating me like a child I'll scream."

Elizabeth was still feeling shocked by the news of Keith Parker's resignation, which had shaken the whole staff and given more credence to the rumours about the *Echo*'s future. She knew Campbell Lowrie had had a furious row with Jack Woolley in which he'd refused to take on the role of acting editor. And she could tell from Helen Stevenson's immaculate eye make-up that she'd been crying and had made running repairs during the day. Roy Randall had been raving on about capitalism and had threatened to throw Alastair Wilson out of the window if he so much as mentioned the words "free newspaper". Even the advertising staff were upset. They'd all liked Keith Parker, and most of them had appreciated his general co-operation. No one had seen Arnold Jennings. The advertising director appeared to have had a diplomatic cold and gone home.

They all knew there was to be a board meeting on Friday morning, but most people thought the decision was a foregone conclusion. Alastair Wilson was the only member of the editorial staff who belonged to the

NUJ and he'd rung head office to ask for information about redundancy payments and so on. They hadn't seemed over-concerned, but promised to put the information in the post. Campbell and the others were in the Institute of Journalists, but they hadn't bothered to contact their office. None of them seemed to have the initiative to do anything.

For Elizabeth, the aspiring journalist, the whole thing was a tragedy. In the blackest of black moods, she saw it all as a conspiracy to thwart her ambitions yet again. The same thing had happened when she'd wanted to go to agricultural college, and when she'd tried to go into the fashion business with Sophie Barlow.

Sophie Barlow? Elizabeth reckoned she'd been born with a silver spoon in her pretty mouth. Not only was she very beautiful, but she was also jolly clever. Apart from the jinxed partnership, everything she touched seemed to turn to gold, and now she was a terrific success in London.

"Why can't I be like Sophie?"

Nigel blinked in surprise.

"Where did Sophie suddenly come from?"

Elizabeth looked at him sulkily. She still didn't know whether or not he'd been out with Sophie when she'd rung him from Berlin, but now wasn't the time to pursue the matter.

"Well she's got everything, and here I am – penniless with my career in ruins. It's not that I'm jealous of her or anything like that, but why can't I have just a little bit of her success?"

Nigel counted the empty gin glasses. There were three, and two of them had been doubles.

"I think we've had enough to drink, Lizzie. Why don't we go off to a Chinese and have something to eat? Say goodbye to Nelson."

Without waiting for a reply, he eased her off the stool and steered her towards the door. Outside, the fresh air hit her, and Nigel had to half-support her as they slowly walked the few hundred yards to the House of Mr Chan.

Settled in a discreet alcove, he continued to play the masterful type, and ordered food for both of them without consulting Elizabeth.

"Thank you, Nigel. You're very sweet."

She'd sobered up enough now to know that Nigel was trying hard to please her.

"I'm sorry I'm being such a pain, but I am very unhappy. I was serious about becoming a journalist, you know. It wasn't just another one of my pipe dreams."

Nigel looked at her in some puzzlement.

"Why don't you start at the beginning, Lizzie? You realise you haven't told me what all this is about. Has the editor finally said you can't be a journalist?"

"Oh, Nigel, it's worse than that. They're going to turn the *Echo* into one of those dreadful free giveaway papers and there won't be any journalists on it. I'll never be a reporter now."

Nigel had never seen real tears on Elizabeth's face, and he felt almost overwhelmed by how beautiful she looked in her vulnerability. He wanted to take her in his arms and comfort her, but he knew that wasn't what she needed.

"A free giveaway doesn't sound like Jack Woolley's style. Are you sure you've got the story right, Lizzie?"

To his embarrassment, Elizabeth began to sob. Gently he teased from her the story of the rumours and counter-rumours, culminating in Keith Parker's resignation. Nigel didn't say much, but he looked very thoughtful. He waited until the sobs had subsided and Elizabeth was wiping her eyes with a paper serviette.

"Look, Lizzie, you mustn't laugh because this is a very serious proposition. What if I were to make Mr Woolley an offer for the paper and keep it as it is? Do you think he'd be prepared to do a deal?"

Elizabeth looked at him coldly.

"I am not in the mood for jokes, Nigel."

Nigel protested.

"It's not a joke, Lizzie. I told you I've got some spare cash I want to invest. It's nowhere near enough for me to buy the *Borchester Echo* on my own, but I've got enough contacts in the City to be able to put together a package that might interest Mr Woolley. I hadn't thought about newspapers until now, but it could be quite a nice moneyspinner."

Elizabeth was so used to thinking of the old, penniless Nigel, she hadn't really accepted the fact that he was a success in London. Though still unsure of his seriousness, she adopted the drowning rat principle.

"Do you have any idea how much it would cost to buy the *Echo*? It's probably hundreds of thousands of pounds. Maybe even a million . . ."

"It doesn't matter much to City folk. If it's a sound investment they'll soon find the money . . ."

"Do you mean you really could get enough people together to buy it?"

"Of course I could. That's what we're up to all the time. It shouldn't take too much effort . . ."

"Could you do it before Friday?"

"Crumbs, Lizzie, that's a bit of a tall order. That's the day after tomorrow. I'm not sure I could put a good presentation together in that time. I'd need to look at the company books to see what's been happening on the old balance sheet over the last year or two. Mr Woolley and his friends would have to be jolly co-operative."

Elizabeth was very excited. She could see the chance of a reprieve. Her journalistic career might be hanging on a thread, but there was still hope. Her mood changed and she was back to her jokey self.

"If you did take over the paper, would you make me the editor?"

"Come off it, Lizzie. You don't think I'm going to prise cash out of those fat cats if they think the paper's not going to have an experienced editor?"

Elizabeth giggled.

"Don't be silly, Nigel. I was only joking. But you would insist there was a place for me in the editorial room somewhere, wouldn't you?"

Nigel was delighted to see her looking perky again.

"If you were nice to me I'd certainly insist that the editor chappie gave you a chance as a copy boy. That's what they call juniors, isn't it?"

Elizabeth gave him a dig in the ribs.

"I don't want to be a copy boy or even a copy girl. I want to be a reporter. I'd settle for a trainee's job, mind you."

Nigel massaged his tender ribs and laughed.

"Right, well that's settled. I become proprietor of the *Borchester Echo*, and you become my most junior reporter. There's only one condition . . ."

Elizabeth could guess the condition, but she wasn't ready for marriage yet. Not with a new career about to be launched.

"Gentlemen don't make conditions, Mr Pargetter. Besides, what would you say to Sophie?"

"Sophie? Oh, all right let's forget the conditions. What next? When do you think I could get to see Jack Woolley?"

Elizabeth looked at her watch.

"It's not quite nine o'clock. If we skip the rest of the meal we could go to Grey Gables and see him this evening."

Nigel took a deep breath. Things were moving fast even by City standards but he wasn't sure whether he was ready to beard the lion in his den yet.

"I'm not sure that it's a good idea to just barge in on him. We ought to ring and make an appointment through Caroline. Let's leave it until first thing in the morning. I'll get on to it straight away then."

Elizabeth's bottom lip dropped.

"You're changing your mind already. That's beastly of you. You've only been having me on all the time. I think that's horrid of you, Nigel Pargetter."

Nigel was hurt.

"I wasn't having you on, Lizzie. I'm deadly serious. I just don't think nine or ten o'clock at night is the time to try to do business with someone like Jack Woolley."

"I thought all you big shots in the City were used to making deals twenty-four hours a day since Big Bang . . ."

"That's true, Lizzie, but we don't usually do it by barging into a chap's private home. It's all done by computer . . ."

"Spare me the economics lesson, Nigel. Grey Gables is a club. It's not the same as just going up to his front door and asking if he'd like to sell us his newspaper. We can go to the club for a drink and bump into him quite casually . . ."

"But Lizzie . . ."

"Please, no buts. We've got to strike while the iron's hot . . ."

"If you ask me it's a bit too jolly hot . . ."

"If we leave it until the morning you won't even get an appointment. Caroline Bone would think you were back in the swimming-pool business again."

Nigel hadn't drunk as much courage as Elizabeth, but he found himself being dragged along by her enthusiasm and determination. He hadn't the heart to tell her he'd never actually made an offer for a company before.

When they arrived at the country club he was very relieved to see that Jack Woolley wasn't in the bar or restaurant.

"That's a shame, Lizzie. It looks as if we've had a wasted journey."

But Elizabeth wasn't ready to give up.

"You wait here, Nigel. I'll go and see if Caroline's in her room."

Caroline lived in the garden suite in the residential side of the club, and Elizabeth was relieved to see a light on. She rang the bell and waited. After a few minutes Caroline appeared, wearing a bathrobe and a towel wrapped around her head.

"Elizabeth, what are you doing here? Come in and make yourself comfortable while I dry off. As you can

132

see, I was in the shower when you rang the bell. Help yourself to a drink."

She disappeared, leaving a trail of damp footprints on the carpet, and came back dressed in a grey tracksuit.

"This is a surprise, Elizabeth. To what do I owe this pleasure?"

Caroline was a close friend of Shula's, but she and Elizabeth had never had much to do with each other. Certainly, casual visits weren't part of their normal social pattern. Elizabeth had taken her at her word and was halfway through a gin and tonic. Her words were slightly slurred.

"Nigel and I need your help . . ."

Caroline's heart sank. Every time she came across Nigel Pargetter it usually meant some kind of trouble.

"We've got to see Mr Woolley urgently."

Caroline eased the glass of gin out of Elizabeth's hand.

"What do you mean by 'urgently'?"

"Now! We have to see him right away . . ."

"Elizabeth, it's ten o'clock at night. Mr Woolley will be in bed by now. And if he's not in bed, he'll certainly be ensconced in his room with a glass of malt whisky. You won't be able to see him tonight. What on earth is it all about anyway?"

Elizabeth couldn't contain herself any longer.

"We want to buy the *Borchester Echo* . . ."

Caroline couldn't believe her ears. She wondered how much the younger girl had been drinking.

"Elizabeth, you can buy a *Borchester Echo* in any newsagent in the county. Admittedly, not at ten o'clock at night, but however proud Mr Woolley may be of his paper he doesn't keep personal supplies here at Grey Gables. You'll just have to wait until the morning."

There was a knock on the door and Caroline opened it to find Nigel, who'd got bored sitting at the bar. She looked at him in dismay, but had to invite him in. Her flat was suddenly a madhouse.

"I don't know what you two have been up to, but I suggest I get you some very strong coffee. You both need to sober up, and then we'll decide whether or not you can drive or should go home by taxi."

Nigel looked puzzled.

"We haven't been up to anything. Hasn't Lizzie explained? We need to see Mr Woolley as soon as possible . . ."

"Oh, yes, she explained all that. She said you needed to see him because you wanted to buy a *Borchester Echo*. Very funny. Ha, ha! I strongly suggest you don't test Mr Woolley's sense of humour in the same way. He's not as polite as I am."

Nigel laughed.

"You've got it wrong, Caroline. We don't want to buy a copy of the paper. We want to buy the actual paper . . . lock, stock and barrel . . ."

"What do you mean, you want to buy it? Buy the *Borchester Echo*? You and Elizabeth? You're out of your minds. You've been drinking too much gin. It's addled your brains. How on earth could you buy the newspaper? It's not for sale anyway? What are you talking about? This is all crazy."

Nigel looked at her patiently and suggested she poured herself a drink while he explained. By the time he was finished Caroline had drunk most of a very large gin and tonic.

"I still think you're mad. In the first place I don't think Mr Woolley's going to go along with the idea of converting the paper to an advertising sheet – that's totally confidential information, mind you. I'm also positive he won't be interested in any offer to buy the paper, and if you'll forgive my saying so, especially from you, Nigel!"

Nigel didn't need any reminders of the trouble he'd got into when he'd tried to sell Mr Woolley a swimming-pool.

"I'm not sure you're right there, Caroline. Don't forget he's a self-made man. He likes to see people get on in the world, especially when it's through their own efforts. I suspect he'll take me more seriously than you think."

Elizabeth nodded in agreement. Caroline was not convinced. But then it suddenly struck her that an offer to buy the paper might just strengthen Mr Woolley's hand at Friday's board meeting. He wouldn't have to say it was an offer from Nigel Pargetter. He could say it was from a group of City businessmen. If Nigel and Elizabeth were to be believed, that was true anyway.

"All right, you two. I'll do it. I'll ring Mr Woolley right now . . . but only because I've had much too much to drink."

She picked up the phone and when she asked to be put through to Mr Woolley's suite she could almost see the porter glance at the clock. Mr Woolley's gruff voice came on the line and she took a very deep breath. Apart from regular enquiries about how much she'd had to drink, Jack Woolley didn't say very much as she re-told the story, prompted from time to time by Nigel and Elizabeth. When she eventually mentioned Nigel's name she held the receiver away from her ear, but instead of the expected roar all she heard was a quiet chuckle.

"The young pup. He thinks he's made enough money to buy out Jack Woolley, does he? You tell him from me . . . no, don't. I'll tell you what, Caroline. Why don't you bring him and young Elizabeth Archer up to my suite and I'll tell him myself?!"

Caroline put down the telephone and looked at the two anxious faces.

"Don't ask me why, but it would seem that the redoubtable Jack Woolley has a weak spot. We are cordially invited to join him for drinks in his private apartment."

Elizabeth looked apprehensive. Nigel was terrified.

"Oh lord, you don't mean now?"

"Yes, I do. Right this very moment. Come on you two. You've started something and now you've got to see it through to the bitter end."

Jack Woolley was wearing a deep-burgundy smoking jacket and had a glass of malt whisky in his hand.

"Come in. It's nice to see you Elizabeth, Nigel. Thank you for bringing them along, Caroline. Sit down everybody. Can I offer you a drink? I'm afraid I only keep my best malt up here, but if that doesn't suit I can get anything you want sent up."

All three said they'd drunk too much already. They were probably right. Nigel sat on the edge of his chair.

"It's jolly decent of you to see us, Mr Woolley. We . . . er . . . didn't realise it was quite so late . . ."

"Think nothing of it, Nigel. A good businessman is happy to talk business any time of the day or night. Maybe that's why so many of us suffer from heart disease!"

Everyone laughed nervously.

"Caroline's given me the bare bones of your proposal. It's very interesting. Is that what you've been hovering about, trying to tell me for the last week or so, Elizabeth?"

Elizabeth was startled that Mr Woolley had even noticed her fruitless attempts at waylaying him.

"Oh, no. Good heavens, no. That was about something completely different . . ."

"What was that?"

"Ah, well . . . er . . . it was before the news about the paper's future broke. I wanted to ask you if there was any chance of reinstating the old agricultural correspondent's job . . ."

"That's funny, Elizabeth. You and Keith Parker must be on the same wavelength. He was talking to me about that only this morning. We'll have to see. Now what about this other proposition? What sort of figure were you thinking of offering me, Mr Pargetter?"

Nigel shuffled uncomfortably.

"We hadn't actually got down to precise figures yet, Mr Woolley . . ."

"No, no, of course not, but what sort of ballpark are we in?"

"Er . . . truthfully I have no idea. This was . . . er
. . . just intended to be an exploratory discussion to see
if you . . . the company . . . might be susceptible to an
outside offer. We'd need to see some accounts before
we were able to make a proper offer, as it were . . ."

"Who would be making this offer?"

"Um . . . it's not easy to be too precise about actual
people. I've still got a fair amount of work to do on the
project . . . talk to a few people . . . throw the idea
around."

"You're not wasting my time by any chance? This
isn't some idea off the top of your head when you've
had too much to drink, and young Elizabeth here has
been worrying out loud about her future?"

Nigel looked at his shoes. They badly needed
cleaning.

"I'm sorry, Mr Woolley. It might seem a bit like that,
and it did just come up this evening as you suggest. But
it's not the way it seems. I do have a little money of my
own to invest, and I'd be approaching some very
reputable contacts in the City so we could put a
package offer together. This is all very premature
because we knew you had a board meeting on Friday,
and we wanted to talk to you before the die was cast."

Elizabeth nodded in agreement.

"That's the truth, Mr Woolley. It's my fault we're
here now. Nigel did want to sort things out properly
and make an appointment to see you in your office. I
just thought all that would take too long and it would
be too late."

Jack took a long, slow sip of whisky.

"Don't worry, Elizabeth. It isn't too late. Quite a few
people have opened my eyes today. Keith Parker made
me realise what my responsibility as a newspaper-
owner is, and how much local people value the service
the paper provides. I talked to several people and they
all said the same thing. Caroline, in her own way, and
now you and Nigel have convinced me that there's
something special about the *Echo*. I couldn't sell it to

137

you if I wanted to. It isn't really mine. I only hold it in trust for the people of Borsetshire."

Elizabeth wanted to hug him, but she knew that would embarrass him.

"Oh, Mr Woolley, does that mean the paper's safe? That it won't become one of those horrid free sheets?"

Mr Woolley poured himself another glass of whisky.

"No, it doesn't mean that, I'm afraid. As I told the editor this morning, I've got a special meeting with the board of directors on Friday. They know what the meeting's about and I've got to let them discuss whatever offer is being made. They might think it's an offer we can't refuse, and I'd have to accept their decision. Otherwise there's no point in having directors. I've got to let this thing run its course."

He paused and took another sip of whisky.

"Mind you, if one of them so much as disagrees with me I'll sack him on the spot!"

He let out a great roar of laughter, and the other three joined him . . . relief showing on their faces.

"Of course, if that last remark should be repeated anywhere I'd sue for libel."

Elizabeth decided to throw caution to the winds and threw her arms round Mr Woolley's neck, gave him a huge hug and kissed him on the cheek.

"Oh, Mr Woolley, you are a darling. Everyone will be so pleased you're not going to change the paper."

Nigel looked on, feeling awkward. He'd have quite liked to throw his arms round Mr Woolley too, but he guessed the gesture wouldn't be appreciated by the older man. Instead, he held out his hand.

"Can I shake your hand, Mr Woolley? I agree with Elizabeth – you're an absolute brick. Everyone will be delighted with your decision to keep the *Echo* just as it has been for so many years."

Jack Woolley looked at Caroline and they smiled. They both knew one man who wouldn't be delighted. Arnold Jennings could well be looking for a new job on Monday morning.

CHAPTER ELEVEN

The tele-ad girls' night out had barely begun but Elizabeth was already beginning to suffer for her moment of weakness. When she had suggested they all had a drink at the Bull she'd forgotten about Eddie Grundy and her cousin Tony Archer, the village's notorious middle-aged romeos. Now she sat cringing while they tried to chat up the *Echo* trio of Ann Jensen, Jenny Hinds and Liz Cole. Elizabeth had realised the whole thing was a mistake the minute she'd stepped into the pub to be greeted by Eddie Grundy's noisy "Hello, darling". She'd tried to pretend she didn't really know him but that plan fell apart when Tony insinuated himself into the party. Much as she wanted to, she couldn't bring herself to deny that he was a member of her family.

Luckily, none of the girls seemed to mind. They were all glad to be away from the office and the strain of not really knowing about their future. Elizabeth hadn't told anyone about her discussion with Jack Woolley so none of them knew about his determination to keep the paper as it was. Jenny and Liz were giggling at Eddie's jokes, and Elizabeth suspected that Ann saw him and Tony as a source of free drinks for the evening.

The landlord, Sid Perks, was quick to cotton on to Elizabeth's plight and had loudly made mention of Eddie's wife Clarrie and Tony's wife Pat. Neither had taken a blind bit of notice and both had gone on competing for the girls' attention. Elizabeth couldn't make up her mind which of them made her cringe most.

Eddie saw himself as one of Ambridge's characters and worked hard at being a non-conformist. He fancied himself as something of a Country and Western singer and often dressed the part. Elizabeth was grateful for the small mercy that this evening he'd stopped short of wearing his ridiculous cowboy hat with the cow's horns sticking out of the top. She couldn't understand a grown man – especially one fast approaching forty – wanting to look like a star-struck teenager.

Cousin Tony was little better. He was about a month older than Eddie and, with a thickening waistline and thinning hair, he more than looked his age. He'd had a reputation as a ladies' man in his younger days, and clearly still believed in his own publicity. He didn't seem to realise that he was almost old enough to be their father and was busy ogling Jenny Hinds, though he was careful enough to include Ann Jensen in the conversation. Elizabeth couldn't hear his patter, but she knew from experience that he would eventually get round to the joys of organic farming and how he was pioneering brave new experiments to produce the sort of healthy food that growing girls, like Jenny and Ann, needed. She guessed that neither of them would have a clue what he was talking about.

Eddie had already discovered Liz Cole's obsession with the pop world and was regaling her with his experience in the record industry.

"I've made three records, darling."

"Really?"

Liz looked interested.

"Yeah . . . three . . . could have made the big time, me."

"Really? Solo? In a group? Or what?"

"Oh . . . solo, of course."

"What sort of backing group did you have?"

Eddie looked a bit puzzled.

"I didn't have a backing group. It was just me and my guitar."

Elizabeth interrupted.

"Didn't you have a girl partner, Eddie?"

"Ah, well . . . not really a partner. You mean Jolene. She wasn't really a partner. I just let her appear with me because we were sort of friends and I wanted to give her career a bit of a boost."

140

Elizabeth couldn't really remember. She had a feeling the lady in question had been much more than a singing partner, but she didn't pursue it. Liz was more interested in the business side.

"Did you make the charts or didn't they have charts in the olden days?"

Eddie ignored the dig about his age . . . or perhaps he didn't notice it.

"Oh, yes. I made the charts all right, darling."

Elizabeth looked at Eddie and raised her eyebrows. He almost blushed.

"To be honest I really only made it with one of them."

Liz was losing interest but she tried to keep the conversation going.

"Which chart was it? NME or Radio One or what?"

"Er . . . no. It wasn't any of them . . . um . . ."

Elizabeth couldn't resist adding to Eddie's discomfort.

"Oh it was much more important than any of the regular charts, wasn't it Eddie?"

"Well, now that you mention it, I suppose it was really."

Eddie could never see Elizabeth's traps.

"It was a specialist one for Country and Western records."

Liz looked disappointed. Her mother was the family's only Country and Western fan.

"Really?"

Elizabeth resisted the temptation to rub salt in Eddie's wounds by revealing that the "chart" in question had been the *Echo*'s own listing of the discs sold in Borchester shops. She'd been away at boarding school at the time but she remembered Shula mentioning it in one of her rare letters. Eddie had won some kind of contract to make more records and tour the London clubs. It had been one of Ambridge's nine-day wonders . . . which, if she remembered correctly, was about as long as the contract lasted. The local boy hadn't made so good and had come home with awful tales about the crooks in the recording business. He had never noticed the irony of the song's title . . . "Lambs to the Slaughter". But his experiences hadn't stopped him making another two records and taking every opportunity to burst into song.

"I still do gigs at the Borchester Country and Western Club, you know. I could get you free tickets if you ever fancied coming along to see me."

Before Liz's disdain for the small time was able to manifest itself, Ann Jensen quickly interrupted to seize on the invitation . . . and, no doubt, to escape from Tony Archer's conversation about organic farming.

"If I came could I bring a boyfriend with me?"

Eddie looked disappointed but rose to the occasion.

"Boyfriend? You won't need no boyfriend there, darling. The place is always full of handsome blokes like me."

Ann fluttered her eyelashes.

"Yes, but surely none of you would be interested in a plain little thing like me?"

For once, Eddie was nonplussed. Underneath all the bravado and loudness, he was a kind-hearted soul. Ann Jensen's morale obviously needed boosting and she wouldn't get that from his noisy banter. He turned on his quieter personality . . . the one usually reserved for Clarrie and the kids.

While all this was going on, Tony Archer had bought two rounds of drinks . . . white wine and soda for Elizabeth; Cinzano and lemonade for Liz; sweet martini for Jenny; and a Bloody Mary for Ann Jensen. The second time around, he had studiously avoided buying another pint of Shires for Eddie but Eddie was much too thick-skinned to take the hint that it was his turn. In fact he complained so loudly about being left out that Sid Perks quickly pulled another pint and added it to Tony's bill.

The bar was busy and there were quite a few strangers among the locals. Sid was anxious not to let anyone get the impression that it was a rowdy place. He knew it would be easier to deal with a slightly disgruntled Tony Archer than the unpredictable Eddie Grundy. He'd had to ban him from the Bull several times in the past, but like the proverbial bad penny, he kept turning up again.

With her second glass of wine and soda, Elizabeth was beginning to feel less anxious about her guests. They all seemed to be perfectly happy. None of them protested in any way about the attentions of Eddie and Tony and, to her surprise, she saw Jenny Hinds smile when a man sitting at one of the other tables winked at her. Elizabeth didn't recognise him and assumed he wasn't from Ambridge. She was just starting to feel gently bored with the evening when the door opened and Nigel Pargetter arrived.

"Lizzie, my darling . . . what a lovely surprise . . . I didn't expect to see you here this evening."

He didn't want to say that he'd been looking for her all over Borchester and had come to the Bull in desperation. He didn't need to. Elizabeth recognised his lap-dog look but for once she didn't mind. She saw all three girls look him over with approval.

"Hello, Nigel. I was hoping to have a quiet evening out with my colleagues from the office but I think I may have brought them to the wrong place for that."

Nigel switched from lap-dog to hangdog.

"Terribly sorry, Lizzie. I don't want to interrupt. You carry on with your chums. Just ignore me. I'll have a quiet drink and a bit of a chat with Sid Perks."

Elizabeth might have let him do just that, but Ann Jensen came to his rescue.

"Aren't you going to introduce us, Elizabeth?"

Soon Nigel had all the girls roaring with laughter over his stories of the City and, to Elizabeth's embarrassment, their ice-cream war.

"Lizzie was ever so sharp at finding all the right pitches and I have to admit she out-manoeuvred me most of the time. She certainly sold a lot more ice-cream than I did . . . as our esteemed boss never ceased pointing out."

Ann Jensen in particular was enjoying the story.

"I can't see you in a Ms Snowy hat, Elizabeth. Didn't it ruin your hair-do?"

Elizabeth could quite cheerfully have strangled Nigel at that point. It was Eddie Grundy who prevented violence. He was fed up with playing second fiddle to Nigel Pargetter and decided it was his turn to needle Elizabeth.

"Heard anything about your soldier boy lately?"

"Do you mean my cousin?"

"Terry Barford ain't your cousin. Nobody goes off for a dirty weekend in Berlin with their cousin. He's only related to you through a second-hand marriage."

The three girls from the *Echo* were agog. They sensed scandal and possibly a public row. Then Nigel disappointed them by climbing on his white charger and pointing the tip of his lance at Eddie.

"Steady on, old chap. There's no point casting aspersions in Lizzie's direction. By your standards she's as pure as the driven snow."

To her surprise, her real cousin – Tony Archer – added his support.

"Yes, watch it Eddie. You're on dangerous ground. You wouldn't want your Clarrie hearing about some of your escapades with Dolly Tredgold, Jolene Rogers and the rest of them!"

Back at the centre of attention, Eddie was unperturbed by the criticisms although he did change tack.

"So what about this career of yours in journalism, then? It didn't last long, did it?"

He was referring to the few weeks when Elizabeth had been allowed to fill in for Alastair Wilson. She'd made the mistake of boasting about it and when nothing had come of it she'd had to swallow her pride in public. Trust Eddie Grundy to find a raw nerve.

"What do you mean, Eddie? I'm still being considered for any job that might come up."

"Yeah . . . I believe you."

Elizabeth was half embarrassed and half angry. She didn't like being shown up in front of the girls.

"I'm working on a story at this very moment."

Before she could stop herself, she'd blurted out her suspicions about the shady antique dealer and some of the steps she'd been taking to track him down. Jenny Hinds listened with interest.

"One of my neighbours is in the antique business. Maybe he could help you? As a matter of fact, that's him at that other table."

She pointed to the man Elizabeth had seen winking at her earlier.

"His name's Foster."

Nigel Pargetter choked on his drink and Elizabeth nearly fell off her stool.

"Not Alan Foster?"

"Yes, it is. Why? Do you know him?"

Elizabeth tried to cover her confusion and excitement.

"Oh, no. I don't know him but I know the name because he rings in with ads now and again. Haven't you taken some from him yourself?"

"Oh, I remember now. He never gives me the ads. He always asks for you. He obviously likes your posh voice. Would you like to meet him?"

Elizabeth looked at Nigel but he only stared back with a blank look.

"Er . . . not right now. Perhaps a bit later. I've suddenly remembered I've got to make a phone call."

Elizabeth needed advice. She rang Helen Stevenson.

"Helen, I've found Alan Foster!"

She explained the coincidence of Foster being in the bar and Jenny Hinds knowing him. Helen was cautious.

"I think you ought to meet him and see how he reacts, but I wouldn't be inclined to ask him any pointed questions at this stage. There's no need to rush, now that we know he lives near Jenny."

As she hung up, Elizabeth found Nigel standing behind her.

"I say, Lizzie, this is a real stroke of luck . . . finding old Foster like this. What shall we do now?"

She told him what Helen had said, and he looked disappointed.

"That's silly. We can't just let him go like that. It's taken ages to track him down . . ."

"We didn't track him down. He's fallen into our laps."

"Well . . . whatever, we've got him in our sights and we ought to strike while the iron's hot."

"I hope I don't mix metaphors like that if I ever get to write this story."

"Come on, Lizzie, never mind the English lesson. What are we going to say to him?"

Elizabeth was uncertain. Like Nigel, her instincts were to tackle him on the spot before he could think of a cover-up story. She could see the headline: "Reporter confronts crooked dealer". On the other hand, she was aware of Helen's experience and she couldn't ignore her advice lightly.

"Do you mind if I ring Nelson and Robin to see what they think?"

Nigel shrugged his shoulders noncommittally. He would have preferred to have been a lone hero but he knew better than to try to stop Elizabeth doing what she wanted. Nelson took Helen's view . . . caution was important. Robin's phone was engaged and Elizabeth became agitated as she tried to get through. She expected to see Alan Foster walk out of the pub and into the night before she could do anything. Eventually Robin answered. He was pleased to hear from her and caught some of her excitement.

"Well, I actually agree with Nigel for once. I think you ought to talk to him tonight. Why don't you stall for about half an hour and I'll buzz over in the Porsche to provide some back-up?"

Back in the bar, Eddie Grundy was still in a belligerent mood.

"You two have been away a long time . . . been having a quick snog out the back, have you?"

146

This high-quality banter continued, with Nigel trying to keep Eddie in check without making him angry. Elizabeth was also conscious of Sid Perks keeping a careful eye on the situation. He knew Eddie could spell trouble. Robin arrived after what seemed like a lifetime but couldn't have been more than half an hour. She'd forgotten that the girls had seen him before – when he was pretending to be someone else – so she was bewildered when they called him Sebastian. He grinned and winked at her.

"It was that day I winkled you out of the clutches of Morgan the Gorgon . . . I told her I was Sebastian, your boyfriend's brother. Remember?"

Behind them, Alan Foster rose and left the bar. Elizabeth was flustered until she noticed that his friend had stayed behind. He'd only gone to the loo! While he was out, she mentioned him to Jenny Hinds and said she would quite like to meet him.

"He's ever such a nice man, Elizabeth. He's lived on our estate for years and he's always been very friendly with my dad. They go drinking together."

"How long has he been in the antique business, Jenny?"

"Not that long. He used to work in a factory or something but then he was made redundant and was on the dole for a long time. I think he started dealing in junk some time last year but he got a bit worried about the council and moved up market to antiques."

"What do you mean? Why should he be worried about the council?"

"I suspect he was worried that one of the neighbours would split on him because there was always junk in his front garden and it made the place look very scruffy. By going into antiques, he probably thought no one would tell the council because it wasn't such a nuisance."

Robin was just as puzzled as Elizabeth.

"Slow down, Jenny. Why should the council care about him being in the antique business? What's it got to do with them?"

Jenny looked at him in surprise.

"Well, you're not allowed to run a business from a council house."

Elizabeth saw her story disappear.

"Do you mean it's illegal to operate a business from where Mr Foster lives . . . in a council house?"

"Yes, of course . . . that's why he doesn't advertise openly."

"You mean, that's why he uses box numbers?"

"I expect so. You won't say anything about it, will you? I'd hate to be responsible for him getting thrown out of his house or having to go back on the dole!"

"Don't worry, Jenny, I shan't say a word . . . to anyone."

Elizabeth looked at Robin and Nigel.

"Could either of you gentlemen get me a very large drink, please?"

They nearly fell over each other in their rush to the bar. They knew how close they had all been to making complete fools of themselves. Elizabeth was relieved that she'd live to do that another day!

CHAPTER TWELVE

There was a strange atmosphere in the *Echo* offices on Monday morning. The board meeting on the Friday had formally decided against changing the style of the paper, but the absence of Keith Parker from the editor's chair destroyed any sense of jubilation. On the editorial floor, there was a feeling that their boss had been the sacrifical lamb, and for no good reason. No one could understand why he'd had to resign. Once he'd been reassured that the paper wasn't going to be full of advertisements, Campbell Lowrie had reluctantly agreed to stand in until a new man could be appointed, but he wasn't a natural leader and could do little to restore morale.

In the main advertising office, most people were keeping a low profile. Arnold Jennings had been expected to resign, but hadn't. He'd been able to rationalise the situation in his own mind and felt no pangs of conscience. He thought Jack Woolley and the board had made the wrong decision, but he'd accepted the majority view and had quickly knuckled down to getting on with his job.

For Elizabeth and the tele-ad girls, life was very much back to normal . . . the normal which was Brenda Morgan at her worst! She prowled around the telephones watching everything that was going on, and snapping at the slightest error. Nobody needed to say she'd fallen out with her boyfriend.

Although she knew she should be pleased that the *Echo* was continuing as a proper newspaper, Elizabeth felt depressed. Every caller seemed more boring than the last – pram for sale . . . little-used baby's cot . . . large quantity of children's toys . . . maternity dress (worn only twice) . . . bicycle (suit boy or girl of ten) – the mothers of Borchester had obviously been in a spring-cleaning mood over the weekend, and were trying to raise a few pounds from their junk. Much more of this, she thought, and even the accounts department might make a nice change.

Across the room she saw Jenny Hinds signalling to her. She got the message and switched a call from Jenny's phone to her own. It was Alan Foster. She blushed at the thought of how close she'd been to a very embarrassing situation.

"Hello, Mr Foster. We haven't heard from you for some time . . . business not doing too well?"

He sounded quite cheerful and assured her that things were going very nicely. When he'd finished giving her no fewer than six separate ads, he was still in a chatty mood.

"By the way, I don't know whether it's of interest to any of your reporters, but I've been asked to do a house clearance that seems to have a bit of a mystery attached to it. Nobody knows who owns the house or the furniture, but apparently it's all original stuff that hasn't been used for forty or fifty years."

Elizabeth looked behind her. For once Brenda Morgan wasn't in the room.

"I'm not supposed to take messages for the news staff, but if you give me the address, I'll certainly pass it on to the editor."

At lunchtime, she managed to get past his dozy secretary and speak to Robin personally. He sounded quite friendly and readily joked about the discovery of Alan Foster's innocence. He suggested they met for a drink, and Elizabeth agreed to see him at Nelson's later in the week. On her way back to the office she thought about Alan Foster's intriguing message, and went up the extra floor to see Roy Randall or Campbell Lowrie. Both were still at lunch. Only Alastair Wilson was there, tapping out a story on a dilapidated typewriter. He stopped and smiled at Elizabeth.

"Hello, gorgeous, come to see a professional at work?"

Elizabeth had never been very keen on Alastair. His super-enthusiasm could be rather wearing. According

150

to him, every story he was sent to cover deserved a place on the front page, and Roy Randall had nicknamed him "Scoop". Elizabeth was even less impressed with him since his comments about free newspapers, and she was inclined to keep the message to herself until someone else came in. However, Alastair beckoned her over to his desk.

"Come and see this story. It's terrific. Campbell's bound to want it for the front page."

Elizabeth looked over his shoulder at the paper in the typewriter.

"Borchester police are this week looking for a toothless burglar. He left a complete set of dentures behind after breaking and entering a shop in Crown Street on Friday night."

Alastair looked at her expectantly.

"It's a great intro, isn't it?"

It certainly made Elizabeth smile so she happily agreed. She remembered the feeling of excitement when she'd written what she felt was a good intro for the few stories she'd been allowed to do in the past.

"By the way, I've got a message from one of our advertisers. It's some information he said I should give to our star reporter, and at the moment there's absolutely no doubt in my mind who that is. Alastair Wilson this is your story."

When she'd relayed the information, the young reporter seemed singularly unimpressed.

"Doesn't seem to be much of a yarn in that, I'm afraid."

Elizabeth was surprised. The little she'd heard from Alan Foster had left her fascinated.

"Won't you even follow it up?"

Alastair balanced precariously on his chair and looked blasé.

"No, I don't think so. You get a nose for a story, you know, and that just doesn't do anything for mine. Bit of a non-starter, I'm afraid. Never mind – but thank your bloke for the tip. Got to encourage people who bother

151

to tell us things. You never know when they might come up with something really hot."

The phone on Roy Randall's desk rang and Alastair leapt across the room to answer it.

"Newsdesk . . . Alastair Wilson here."

Elizabeth left him to his moment of glory and went downstairs to start another shift of mindlessness . . . four hours of taking down boring tele-ads. The afternoon was even more tedious than she'd expected, and by six o'clock she was sorry she'd put Robin off until later in the week. She could do with a drink. She thought of ringing Nigel, but then remembered he'd gone back to London that morning. As she was leaving, Helen Stevenson came down the stairs behind her.

"Hello, Elizabeth. Are you as pleased as the rest of us about our stay of execution? By the way I never got the chance to thank you for inviting me to supper. I really enjoyed it. I sent your mother some flowers, but I've been meaning to catch up with you personally to say thank you. Where are you off to now? Somewhere exciting?"

Elizabeth shook her head miserably.

"No, I'm afraid not. I was going to stop off at Nelson's for a glass of wine on the way home, but all my friends seem to be unavailable so I'll have to give it a miss."

Helen saw she needed cheering up.

"Not all your friends are unavailable. I'm free. How about joining me for a drink or did you have something a bit more romantic in mind?"

Elizabeth was delighted.

"Oh, no. I'd love to have a drink with you. Maybe we can have a sensible conversation about your agricultural aspirations."

When they got to the wine bar, Elizabeth discovered that Helen had never been there before, so she had the pleasure of introducing her to Nelson Gabriel. Nelson was immediately taken by the beautiful Helen.

152

"Where have you been hiding this delectable creature, young Elizabeth? Why haven't you brought her in to brighten my life before now?"

Once she was satisfied that Helen was amused rather than put off, Elizabeth laughed.

"Just ignore him! He's an old lecher, given half the chance . . ."

"What an outrageous remark for a well-brought-up young lady to make about a man of my impeccable credentials. Please take no notice of her Miss Stevenson . . ."

"*Mrs* . . ."

Helen interrupted with just enough emphasis to make the point.

"I understand perfectly, *Mrs* Stevenson. Now, as you're a first-time patron may I encourage a further visit by offering you a glass of champagne on the house?"

When he brought the champagne Nelson brought three glasses.

"May I share this drink with you, Mrs Stevenson? I won't hover long, I promise. I just want to ask my young friend here how her various investigations are going."

Elizabeth told him about the farce over Alan Foster, while Helen listened with amused interest.

"What a shame it turned out that way. It did seem to have the makings of a good story. By the way, that's not the item you were trying to pass on to Alastair today? He said you'd been up, but the story you'd told him about wouldn't make anything."

Elizabeth shook her head, and then looked guiltily at Nelson.

"Forgive us Nelson, but we did come to talk shop."

Nelson faded quickly into the background, leaving the champagne bottle in an ice-bucket.

"No, as I was saying Helen, I talked to Alastair about another story, but funnily enough it came from the antique dealer we've just been talking about."

She related Alan Foster's message.

"In a way I'm glad there isn't a story in it because I'd have felt guilty if he'd put us on to something interesting when we'd been trying to shop him."

Helen couldn't help laughing.

"You know, Elizabeth, you've got an awful lot to learn about local journalism. It's not the sort of game you've obviously been watching on television . . ."

"But I don't see it like that at all. Honestly, Helen, I am very serious about wanting to become a reporter. Why won't anyone take me seriously? I know I've been a bit of a scatterbrain in the past, and I still say lots of silly things, but I am growing up fast. I know I've got zillions of things to learn, honestly I do."

Helen's lingering doubts disappeared as she looked at the earnestness on Elizabeth's face.

"What you need more than anything else is patience, and I suspect that's not one of your strong points."

She paused long enough to see if she would be contradicted. She wasn't, and she was pleased. Maybe there was a glimmer of hope for the younger girl.

"When I first tried to get into newspapers – and I know it's so long ago that it must seem like the Dark Ages to you – I had to write to dozens and dozens of papers before I even got a reply. I think it was my fifty-second application that got me an interview, and I know it was the sixtieth that got me a job.

"It was a little local paper in East Anglia. They offered me ten guineas a week, and then added another ten and sixpence because I had a couple of A-levels. I had to sign indentures that committed me to them body and soul for three years, and I spent my first six months making tea and going to funerals. I used to have to stand in the pouring rain asking the mourners for their names, and trying to read the messages on the sodden wreath cards. It didn't seem to have much to do with journalism at the time."

If she thought she was depressing her young friend she was wrong. Elizabeth's eyes were brighter than ever.

"You don't understand, Helen. I'd give my eye-teeth for that sort of training. I'm not a starry-eyed kid any more. In a way I've already started my apprenticeship. If you want to know what boredom and mindlessness really are, you should sit taking tele-ads for a few days, but at least it's taught me about the need for accuracy. I've also learned how to think of intros and last paragraphs that can be cut off if the story's too long. Alastair told me all that when I was doing those little stories last year."

Nelson returned with a second bottle. It wasn't champagne, but nor was it Algerian.

"Forgive me for interrupting, but I noticed your bottle was empty and that's a very bad advertisement for a wine bar. I'm prepared to offer you this modest little wine on the house, but of course I wouldn't want to discourage you from *buying* another bottle of champagne if that's the sort of mood you're in."

The girls looked at each other, and in unison ordered champagne. Nelson made a mental note to insist on taxis later in the evening. He had a feeling that neither of them would be in a fit state to drive. As they slowly drank their way through the champagne, the bar had begun to fill up and their ever-increasing laughter was lost in the general hubbub. Elizabeth recounted the story of Nigel's attempts to buy the *Echo* from Mr Woolley, and Mr Woolley sitting in his amazing smoking jacket, sipping best malt whisky and talking about what a hard life he'd had. Helen had tears streaming down her cheeks by the time she finished.

"It's a great pity it didn't come off, Helen, because Nigel would certainly have given me a job on your floor – even if it was only to scrub it!"

She hooted with laughter, and attracted disapproving stares from some of the other customers.

"He'd also have made you our agricultural correspondent or whatever else you wanted to be."

A hand fell on Elizabeth's shoulder and her brother David suddenly appeared.

"I thought it had to be you making all the racket, little sister. How are you Helen? Still aspiring to write about our green and pleasant land?"

Elizabeth tried to get rid of him.

"Please go away, David. We're having a girl-reporter-to-aspiring-girl-reporter talk. There's no room for a male chauvinist contribution, thank you very much. Unless, of course, that contribution was another bottle of bubbly."

David shrugged his shoulders.

"Please yourselves, but I've just come from an NFU meeting. There were some horror stories being told about land prices, and the serious problems some local farmers are getting into because they can't sell the land that has been deregulated."

Through the slight alcoholic haze, Helen was still able to recognise the makings of a good farming story, and she ignored Elizabeth's suggestions that David should remove himself immediately.

Half an hour and a very long technical explanation later, she too was hoping that David would soon disappear from the scene. Her aspirations to write about agriculture and farmers, especially earnest farmers like David Archer, were fast evaporating. Then, thankfully, a young blonde grabbed him by the arm and dragged him back to the party he'd originally been with.

While Helen was being harangued by her brother, Elizabeth had quietly got on with the serious business of counting the bubbles in her glass. Every time she thought she was getting close to a total the glass seemed to be empty.

"I think I'm ever so slightly tipsy. Maybe I'd better not drink any more. What shall we do now?"

Helen stood up to check her own stability. Both her legs were in reasonable working order.

"How far away is this house that your antique man was talking about? If it's not too far maybe we could walk there and have a look at it?"

Elizabeth thought that was a terrific idea, but it was dark outside.

"We won't be able to see anything unless there happen to be a few handy lamp posts . . .

"Come on, Elizabeth. Where's your sense of adventure? You'll never make a reporter unless you learn to be interpid . . . er intrepid. Follow me."

The two girls shouted their goodbyes to Nelson, David and the whole bar, and warily made their way into the street.

Nearly an hour later, they stood outside a very ordinary detached villa standing well back from the road in a little cul-de-sac with only one other house. A single lamp post at the entrance to the street gave only the dimmest of light. Elizabeth was still feeling giggly, but Helen had sobered up.

"Are you sure this is the right house? It doesn't look any different from all the other houses around here . . ."

"How can you tell? I can hardly see a thing?"

"What did Alan Foster tell you about it?"

"Not very much . . . just that there was a mystery."

Elizabeth's giggles stopped and her eyes widened.

"Don't look now, Helen, but I've got an awful feeling that the Borsetshire Constabulary have sent out a posse to apprehend us."

Helen looked round to see the slight figure looming out of the shadows. He switched on his torch.

"All right then, what are you two up to? Oh, it's you. Aren't you from the *Echo*? What's going on?"

Helen sighed with relief. PC Paul O'Brien was one of the young policemen she often saw when she covered cases at the Crown Court.

"We're not up to any no good . . ."

She was conscious of the words coming out in a jumble. Champagne, fresh air and nervousness made a heady mixture. She corrected herself.

"We're not doing anything you need worry about, constable. We heard there was an interesting story about this house and we thought we'd take a peek at it. There's nothing wrong with that, is there?"

Elizabeth stood blinking in the bright torchlight and the young policeman eyed her appreciatively.

"Well, I must say you don't exactly look like a pair of villains close up but you've frightened half the neighbours to death prowling around at this time of night. We've got a Neighbourhood Watch Scheme in this area and we've had three separate calls reporting suspicious characters loitering with intent."

Elizabeth's nervousness disappeared as she saw that the policeman wasn't much older than her.

"We may be alone and palely loitering but our intent is honourable, officer. You can report back to your superiors that there's nothing to disturb the peace or to stop the neighbours going to sleep perchance to dream . . ."

Helen couldn't help laughing at Elizabeth's slurred speech and she was relieved to see that PC O'Brien was smiling too. He held his torch steadily on their faces.

"I could always run you in for being drunk and disorderly . . . creating a nuisance . . . acting in a manner likely to cause a breach of the peace . . . come to that, I might be able to charge you with conspiring to commit a burglary. I'm sure you've got hairgrips or something in your handbags. I could assume they were tools of the trade."

PC O'Brien was enjoying himself.

"It'd look good in the paper. 'PC foils break-in: Two lady burglars caught in act'. I wonder if your editor would appreciate such a good story. It's probably better than the one you've been following up!"

While Elizabeth and Helen contemplated the long list of charges and the possible sentences, PC O'Brien used his personal radio to report back to his station sergeant that there didn't appear to be any problems in the vicinity, but he'd have a quick scout around to make doubly sure.

"Right, that's delayed the arrival of reinforcements for the time being. Let's go and have a closer look at this mystery of yours . . . that's if you don't mind accepting a helping hand from your friendly community policeman."

His powerful torch cut a swathe through the darkness as they walked up the short drive. As the light danced across the front of the house, it revealed no more than a perfectly ordinary red-brick, pre-war villa. The paintwork was in good condition. Neither Helen nor Elizabeth had known what to expect, but they shared the disappointment of the ordinariness of it all. Elizabeth's enthusiasm, however, was far from flagging.

"Could we try looking through one of the windows, do you think?"

Obligingly, the policeman shone his torch across the downstairs windows, but they were all obscured by net curtains.

"You're not going to see much through that lot and before you ask, I'm *not* going to help you effect an entry! You'll have to come back in daylight."

Elizabeth looked as if she might be prepared to push her luck, but Helen gave her a warning shake of the head. As they walked back along the garden path, the policeman shone his torch on the estate agent's "For Sale" sign.

"Why don't you contact them and say you're thinking of buying it?"

Elizabeth looked up at the sign and gave a squeal of delight. The agents were Rodway and Watson . . . and her sister, Shula, worked for the company.

CHAPTER THIRTEEN

With Phil and David safely fed and out in the fields, Jill Archer was quietly enjoying an extra cup of tea when she heard the post van draw up and the cheery shout of the driver as he dropped a small bundle of letters by the back door. She went out to pick up the letters, and Elizabeth came slowly down the stairs – still in her dressing gown and looking decidedly peaky.

"Morning, Elizabeth. You look like the morning after the night before. Where on earth did you get to last night? David said you left Nelson Gabriel's long before him but it must have been well after midnight before you got home."

Elizabeth winced as she spoke.

"Please don't shout, mother. My head is throbbing. I think I must have bumped it on the ceiling when I woke up this morning."

Jill Archer laughed. Her youngest daughter's sense of humour seldom deserted her and made it difficult to be angry with her for long.

"If I were you, I'd get dressed and have your breakfast quickly before your father gets back. He's livid with you for banging the door when you got in last night. He couldn't get back to sleep again."

Two cups of coffee and several pieces of toast later, Elizabeth was beginning to feel a bit more human, and noticed that one of the letters on the table was for her. It was from Terry Barford. He hadn't wasted much time since their Berlin weekend. She thought she had a few minutes in hand to read it but when she heard her father coming into the yard she grabbed the letter and fled upstairs to escape his wrath. If she could keep out of his way until the evening, she hoped he'd forget her tipsy interruption of his beauty sleep.

Once safely upstairs, she looked at the envelope, and was surprised to see that the sender was SERGEANT Terence Barford. Terry must have had another promotion and he hadn't even mentioned it when they were together! He was going to die of modesty one of these days, she thought. She looked at her watch and realised she was going to be late if she didn't rush. The letter would just have to wait until later. She propped it up on her dressing-table and hurried through the routine of showering, dressing and adjusting her face for the rigours of another day spent listening to the inanities of people wanting to sell their rubbish to other inane people. She'd much rather have followed up the story that she and Helen Stevenson had set out to unravel the night before, but that would have to wait.

As she crashed the gears in her car, the throbbing in her skull increased in tempo, and she vowed yet again not to go drinking at Nelson Gabriel's wine bar in the middle of the week. Her frail body wasn't up to such constant punishment. She drove out of the farm, ignoring her father who was crossing the yard and waving angrily at her. Pretending not to notice, she accelerated away from more aggravation.

She got to the office with only seconds to spare before she would have found herself in Brenda Morgan's bad books for the rest of the day. As it was, the supervisor settled for an extremely cool "Good morning" and an unsympathetic glare. For Elizabeth, the morning was punctuated by shadowy figures attacking her fragile brain with chainsaws and power-drills. She hadn't expected to live until lunchtime and was therefore surprised to see Helen Stevenson, her partner in crime, come into the office. Helen showed no sign of the wear and tear of the previous night's drinking and her elegance made Elizabeth feel almost cross.

"You look disgustingly well. Why can't you have the grace to look at least half as bad as I feel?"

Helen smiled.

"Ah, young Lizzie, by the time you get to my ripe old age, you'll find that the body can absorb much more punishment than you could ever imagine. Besides, the scent of a good story is the best cure I know for a hangover."

Elizabeth groaned at her cheerfulness but perked up at the mention of the story.

"Do you really think we're on to something, Helen?"

Helen nodded, a trifle more gently than necessary for someone who claimed not to be feeling fragile.

"I'm sure of it. While you've been playing at tele-ads this morning, I've been doing a little digging around myself. I've talked to some of the neighbours and none of them can ever remember seeing anyone living there, although the garden has been tended regularly. All the paintwork is in very good repair and, again, nobody seems to know who's kept it that way. It's all very odd. One old dear is convinced that it's the hideout of a Nazi war criminal or Howard Hughes!"

Elizabeth looked puzzled.

"Who's Howard Hughes?"

A tiny crack appeared in Helen's elegant facade.

"Cruel youth. You are joking, aren't you? You can't be so young that you don't know about one of the world's most famous recluses?"

"I'm sorry, but I'm afraid I've never heard of him."

Elizabeth really was apologetic. She didn't want the age difference to become a barrier, but she needn't have worried. Helen was apparently unconcerned.

"Never mind about Howard Hughes. I've also taken the liberty of using your name at Rodway and Watson's, and your sister put me on to the man who's actually handling the sale. We've got a date with him in half an hour . . . and what's more, the acting editor – darling old Scotsman that he is – has arranged with your supervisor for you to have an extra hour for lunch!"

Elizabeth looked across at Brenda Morgan in disbelief. To her astonishment, the supervisor gave a weak smile and nodded in an attempt at an approving manner.

"Gosh, thank you Miss Morgan . . . Brenda. That's really super of you. I do appreciate it. I'll work late to make up for it. I promise."

Brenda Morgan enjoyed this bit of grovelling and preened herself.

"That's quite all right, Elizabeth, we all work for the same newspaper and it would be a poor show if the different departments couldn't help each other out from time to time."

Elizabeth assumed the dragon must be in love again and silently thanked Eros, Cupid . . . and the unfortunate lover! On the way out, she asked if Helen had heard any news about Keith Parker.

"I spoke to him this morning. To be honest, in my 'morning after' state I'd forgotten that he'd resigned and I really rang him to talk about your story. I remembered just as he answered the phone. We didn't talk for long but he seemed all right."

"Has he got a new job lined up?"

Helen shook her head.

"He said he wasn't interested in another editor's job. Apparently he'd had an offer to go into partnership with an old mate in the public relations business and he was seriously thinking about taking it up."

Elizabeth didn't know anyone in the PR world but she knew the reputation PR people had with journalists.

"That doesn't sound like a good idea for someone like him."

"No, you're right, but he said it was just a way of making some money so he can eventually do the things he wants to do . . . which include taking time off to go round the world and write the odd book or two."

"Gosh . . . here's me busting a gut to get into the newspaper world and Keith can quite cheerfully walk out of it overnight. There's no justice."

When Elizabeth and Helen arrived at the house in Ambridge Lane, a smart young man in a tweed sports jacket was already trying to open the front door and seemed to be having some trouble. He turned to greet them.

"Hello, I'm Ian Davies of Rodway and Watson. You must be the young ladies from the *Echo*. I'm afraid whoever painted this door did the most awful job. It's obviously been done with the door closed and I can't get it open now."

Helen and Elizabeth looked at him in dismay, both thinking they were at the mercy of a wimp. They were wrong. Like the well-scrubbed boy scout he looked, he took out a penknife and quickly ran it along the top of the door, then down both sides. It took him several minutes to cut through the layers of paint, but he seemed unconcerned about the damage.

When he tried the lock again, a hefty push succeeded in dislodging the door from its frame. As he pushed it fully open, a wave of stale air assailed them. Elizabeth and Helen looked at each other, not quite knowing what to do next. The smell was almost overwhelming and they were both afraid of what they might find. Ian Davies tried to switch on a light and swore when he realised there was no electricity.

"I hope you two have got good eyesight. It's very gloomy in there."

Beyond the tiny hall, a door led into the murky gloom of the kitchen, where they could see that the table had been laid for breakfast. One knife and fork lay alongside a single plate, stained with the remains of long-rotted food. A tiny jug had a horrible crust of what had once been milk in the bottom, and a thick layer of grimy dust covered everything. Helen was the first one to spot a neatly folded newspaper which lay on one of the chairs. It was brown with age, and she picked it up and looked at the date.

"My God. It's dated 2nd October . . . 1943."

Elizabeth looked over her shoulder in amazement.

"You don't think this has all been left here for the past forty-five years, do you?"

Ian Davies, who'd been poking around in the cupboards, held up a rusted tin with the words "dried eggs" barely legible on the faded label.

"This is all wartime stuff in the cupboard. There's lots of things . . . powdered milk, tinned potatoes . . . even spam. It certainly looks as if nothing's been disturbed for absolute yonks."

Helen looked excited.

"What an amazing discovery! There simply must be a fascinating story behind this. You're on to a real winner, Elizabeth."

Elizabeth looked at her with a mixture of delight and fear . . . delight at Helen's generosity in acknowledging her part in the story; fear at her total lack of experience in handling such a mystery.

"What do we do next?"

"What *you* do next, Elizabeth, is persuade young Mr Davies here to tell you all he knows about this desirable property . . . who owns it, where they are now, why it's been left untouched for so long . . ."

Ian Davies interrupted.

"I certainly wouldn't want to spoil a good story, but I'm afraid there's absolutely nothing I can tell you. I don't know anything."

Both girls looked at him in near-despair. Elizabeth was the first to find her voice.

"You've got to know something. Surely you must know the name of the client who's selling it?"

The young estate agent looked even younger.

"I really haven't a clue. We're handling it on behalf of a firm of London solicitors and I know there's no vendor's name on any of the papers because I looked before I left the office."

Sensing that Elizabeth's frustration was rapidly changing to anger, Helen turned on the charm.

"Don't worry, we'll just have to become detectives. You don't mind if we root around looking for clues, do you Ian?"

Neither of the girls waited for an answer.

Apart from more evidence of wartime food, cutlery and crockery, the kitchen offered little of interest, and they went through into what would have been called the front parlour in the 1940s. Ian Davies followed them but said nothing. His normal ethics had been submerged in the intrigue.

The parlour was sparsely furnished. On the floor was an old-fashioned waxcloth and a single rug in front of a tiny fireplace. The table by the window was covered with a chenille cloth and on it was a huge pot that contained what was left of an aspidistra. Everywhere was the same grimy dust they'd seen in the kitchen. Whoever arranged for the regular gardening and maintenance had clearly avoided letting anyone into the house. A wooden paper rack yielded up yellowed copies of the *Radio Times*, *People's Friend* and *My Weekly*. All of them were dated September, 1943.

It was Elizabeth who discovered the first real clue. Lying flat on the utility sideboard was a silver-framed, tinted photograph of a young couple, both smiling the broad grins of newly-weds. He wore an army uniform with a single subaltern's pip on his epaulette and the girl's hair hung in heavy curls around the collar of a flowered dress. It was a classic wartime picture of a wedding hurriedly arranged before the grooom went off to serve king and country. Helen looked at Elizabeth.

"I wonder if there are any letters or anything around that will tell us more?"

Ian Davies coughed.

"I'm afraid the atmosphere in here is getting to me. If you don't mind, I'll wait for you outside."

When his conscience had been taken out into the fresh air, the two girls decided to look inside the drawers of the sideboard. In the second one Elizabeth opened, there was a cardboard box with a pink ribbon tied round it.

"I think I've found some love letters. Should we go any further, Helen? I feel as if we're intruding on something very private."

Helen Stevenson remembered a few years before when she would have felt the same . . . but too many years as a journalist had blunted the sharp edges of morality. A story was a story was a story. It seemed unlikely that there would be anyone around to complain if they peeped inside the box. They also had the option of dropping the story if they did uncover something too personal for publication.

She took the box from Elizabeth and carefully undid the ribbon. Inside was a neat pile of enevelopes each addressed to "Miss Marjorie Lyttleton, Carlton House, Heydon Lane, Borchester". Helen could hardly believe it. She knew Carlton House. It was the home of one of the town's most prominent citizens . . . Colonel Henry Lyttleton, the former High Sheriff of Borsetshire. A single telephone call to the old boy could clear up the mystery. But she wasn't sure whether or not to leave making the call to Elizabeth. She knew the colonel from his days on the magistrates' bench and he could be either charming or impossible, whichever way the mood took him.

While Helen was pondering what to do, Elizabeth had been reading one of the letters which she'd carefully eased out of the top envelope. It had been signed "Your ever loving Neil".

"It's such a lovely letter, Helen. Neil was obviously madly in love with Marjorie. It's all about how much he's missing her and how much he's looking forward to 15th September . . . their wedding day!"

"What date did you say?"

"15th September."

"Is that 15th September, 1943?"

"Yes."

"I think we've probably done enough prying here, Elizabeth. That paper in the kitchen is dated 2nd October. Let's go back to the office. I think we ought to make all our other enquiries from there, don't you?"

Elizabeth nodded sadly. The tragedy that had befallen the loving couple sometime between their planned wedding and 2nd October hung heavily in the air.

Back in the noisy editorial room at the *Echo*, Helen made the initial call to Colonel Lyttleton. She confirmed that Marjorie had been his younger sister and then, when she was sure he wasn't going to be difficult, passed the telephone over to Elizabeth. After Elizabeth had been talking to the old man for a few minutes, tears began to roll down her cheeks and the other reporters stopped their chattering typewriters. Alastair Wilson looked distinctly uncomfortable. He was beginning to realise just how big a mistake he'd made in ignoring Elizabeth's tip-off about the story.

It was a sad story that unfolded. Neil Hawkins and Marjorie Lyttleton had been childhood sweethearts and had always planned to marry on Marjorie's 21st birthday . . . 15th September, 1943. When Neil joined up and became a lieutenant in the Royal Engineers, it looked as if their plans would have to be postponed. However, a sympathetic CO had granted special permission for the wedding to go ahead on the planned date, only three days before the regiment was sent to Italy.

On 25th September, Lieutenant Hawkins saw his first active service and his conspicuous gallantry in the face of the enemy won him a mention in despatches. He had led his troop through a minefield and blown up a German gun emplacement during the battle to capture Naples.

On 26th September, Lieutenant Hawkins again led his men through a minefield. This time he didn't make it. A mine exploded and ripped off his left leg.

On 1st October, the day Naples finally fell to the Allies, Lieutenant Hawkins died in a field hospital in Italy. He was awarded the Military Cross posthumously.

On 2nd October, the War Office sent a telegram to his widow, Mrs Marjorie Hawkins of 105 Ambridge Lane, Borchester. It arrived while she was eating a solitary breakfast. Later that day, her mother – unable to console the distraught girl – called the family doctor. He could only prescribe a sedative.

Ten weeks later, on 25th December, while Christmas bells were ringing throughout the country, Marjorie Hawkins had been admitted to a psychiatric hospital near Birmingham.

Henry Lyttleton had learned of his sister's condition only when he returned from war service nearly two years later. When he visited her in hospital, he had barely recognised her lifeless face. She hadn't even known he was there. The doctors had told him there was no hope of recovery. His mother and his youngest sister, Margaret, had been told at the outset, but they hadn't believed it. They'd refused to give up hope of her recovery, and Henry Lyttleton hadn't had the heart to argue with them. He was afraid of what that might have done to their own now-fragile minds. From then on, the family had always talked about Marjorie's *temporary* illness, and the house in Ambridge Lane was kept exactly as it had been on the morning of 2nd October, 1943 . . . for the day she was able to return.

On 1st October, 1987, forty-four years to the day after her husband died, Mrs Marjorie Hawkins passed away peacefully in her sleep . . . unaware, as far as anyone could tell, that there had ever been a war or a handsome young lieutenant named Neil. It was only then . . . finally to close the unhappiest chapter in the history of the Lyttleton family . . . that the colonel had instructed his solicitor to dispose of the house. His sister, Margaret, who had devoted most of her life to tending the garden in Ambridge Lane, reluctantly agreed. The "For Sale" sign had been put up a few weeks later.

When he heard the outline of the story, Campbell Lowrie, hard-bitten veteran of Fleet Street, gently installed Elizabeth and Helen in the tiny editor's office and closed the sliding glass door.

"Nobody's to disturb these girls until they're ready to come out. And I mean nobody."

While Helen sat and watched, Elizabeth tapped away at Campbell's ancient typewriter, only stopping to ask how to spell "lieutenant". Helen read each page as it came off the typewriter and was delighted to find that there was nothing she would have wanted to change. When it was finished, Campbell Lowrie glanced at the article.

"Not bad . . . it's not bad at all. I think we'll be able to find a wee place for it all right."

Helen laughed and gave Elizabeth a big hug.

"That, my young friend, almost certainly means you have just written your first front-page story and I'll be very surprised if you don't get a special by-line. This calls for a celebration. Let's go to Nelson's and I'll buy you a bottle of champagne."

Elizabeth wasn't sure whether it was the effort of trying to put everything in the right order or just the emotional impact, but writing the story had drained her, and she suddenly felt very tired.

"I'm sorry, Helen, I'm not really in the mood for drinking. Would you mind very much if I gave it a miss for this evening?"

CHAPTER FOURTEEN

By the time she got home to Brookfield, weariness had settled on Elizabeth and her pallor stilled even her father's irritation. Her mother looked anxious but said nothing when Elizabeth excused herself from the usual pre-supper chatter and went upstairs to lie down. As she took off her shoes, she noticed Terry Barford's letter on the dressing-table. She remembered that other letter from a young soldier and felt the awful sadness of the afternoon wash over her again. Tired as she was, she took the letter from the envelope and began to read it.

Terry Barford clearly didn't have the same eloquence as Lieutenant Hawkins, but after a couple of paragraphs, Elizabeth realised she *was* reading another love letter. There was no great proclamation of undying affection but it didn't need a genius to read between the lines. He was obviously in love with her. She couldn't quite believe it.

Elizabeth had really enjoyed the few days in Berlin. She and Terry always got on well when they were together but they'd never even talked about anything serious. She'd thought they were simply having fun but Terry had obviously seen it differently. In the letter, he said he was sorry they hadn't had more time to talk.

"It was a fabulous weekend for me but I wish it could have been even longer. There was so much I wanted to say to you and in the end, I never got round to saying any of it."

His promotion to sergeant had, he said, made him start thinking about his life and what he wanted to do with it.

"I enjoy the army. It's always very interesting and sometimes quite exciting but there's something missing. I'm not sure this is where I belong any more. I don't feel as if I've got a proper future . . . one with a wife and family. Some of my mates are married and live happily enough in army quarters but their wives are always going on about the next posting and where they'll end up. They never seem settled. I don't think the army's the place for a family. Do you?"

The truth was, Elizabeth had never given the idea any thought at all. In all her flights of fancy, the one perch she'd never touched down on was an army barracks. She had no concept of life in the services and had never stopped to think about the problems of being a soldier's wife. But now she was confronted with it as an option, she knew with total certainty that it was not the life for her. The regimentation of a closed community would stifle her, she was sure.

She lay back and closed her eyes, while her thoughts drifted away from Terry Barford to Robin Fairbrother. Robin was more her idea of the romantic hero. He was always charming and usually good fun. He gave her access to a relaxed lifestyle and to people who appeared to have the same carefree attitudes as him. She enjoyed the champagne life . . . but was Robin's flashy flat – designer-furnished and immaculate but without any trace of fresh air – the place to settle down? There would always be champagne on ice and she couldn't imagine many dull moments with Robin. But could she ever see herself being married to him? What about the shadow of his first wife? Would she be able to live with the knowledge that she was Robin's second choice? For the first time, Elizabeth knew the answer . . . and again with total certainty. It was no.

Inevitably her thoughts moved on to Nigel Pargetter. She liked Nigel enormously. She knew half his dottiness was carefully constructed eccentricity because he couldn't bear to be run-of-the-mill. Underneath it all, he was quite a solid, steady character. He was obviously very successful in the City and despite his Hooray Henry manner, the chances were that he had a very bright future ahead of him. She was sure he could offer her a very comfortable life. He might even become a millionaire . . . but would she want to spend the rest of her life with him? The answer was again quite definitely negative.

Thank you, Terry Barford, she thought. In one fell swoop he had effectively written off both the other men in her life! She went back to his letter.

"What I've been thinking is that I could leave the army at the end of this year and with the bit of cash I've saved over the years, I could get a nice little place in Ambridge. What do you think?"

Elizabeth realised that this was as close to a proposal as poor Terry was ever likely to get. His shyness permeated even his writing. But what about a nice little place in Ambridge? Was that what she wanted for her future? Sadly for him, Terry Barford didn't come into the equation – she'd have to be very careful how she replied to his letter – but what about staying in the village where her family had its roots?

She was the third generation of the Archers at Brookfield Farm but she knew from the family tree in her father's office that their ancestors had been in and around Ambridge for hundreds of years before that. Of course, not everyone had stayed put. Both her grandfather's brothers had emigrated. Great-Uncle Ben had gone to Canada and Great-Uncle Frank to New Zealand. She was always being told about how well they had done in the colonies . . . especially Frank Archer. He'd married a wealthy sheep farmer's daughter and had eventually taken over the huge farm.

When he died, his widow had come to live in Ambridge and, according to local gossip, had splashed her money around a bit too ostentatiously. Elizabeth couldn't remember that, of course. To her, Aunt Laura was just a bossy, eccentric old lady. Before she'd died two or three years earlier, she had teamed up with an ex-army man, Colonel Danby, and they'd kept the odd pig and a few ducks in an attempt at self-sufficiency.

Elizabeth wondered what her Great-Uncle Frank would have made of it all. She'd once asked her grandfather about him and had been surprised by the coolness of his response. Dan Archer, it seemed, had a guilt complex about both his brothers. He felt responsible for their running off to faraway places while he stayed in Ambridge and built up the farm. From what Elizabeth was able to piece together, he might have been right about Ben going away but he'd had nothing to do with Frank's decision. There was some story about Dan and Ben having a fight over her grandmother and the farm with the winner – Dan – taking all. As for Frank, he'd simply gone off to New Zealand rather than join up and fight in the First World War. He'd been a conscientious objector.

Elizabeth loved going back over family history and especially enjoyed any little hints of scandal – not that there appeared to be a great deal of that among the Archers. Most of them seemed to have been honest-to-God country stock and she felt quite happy to follow in their footsteps. But whose footsteps? Should she strike out like her great-uncles and conquer the world, or should she stay at home like her grandfather?

Before she could resolve her dilemma, she heard someone banging at her door. It was David.

"Telephone, Lizzie!"

"Who is it?"

David was his usual co-operative self.

"Don't know . . . didn't ask."

"Male or female?"

"When did you ever get a telephone call from a woman?"

The banter continued all the way down the stairs.

When she picked up the phone, Elizabeth was surprised to hear the gruff tones of Jack Woolley.

"Good evening, Elizabeth, I hope you don't mind me disturbing you at home like this."

She couldn't be sure whether or not that was a barbed reference to her late-night intrusion at Grey Gables earlier in the week.

"Not at all, Mr Woolley."

"Only, I've been thinking about your determination to get into journalism and the terrific commitment you showed when you and young Pargetter said you wanted to buy the *Echo*. It's really very commendable."

Elizabeth didn't know what to say and couldn't imagine what was going to come next. You could never tell with Mr Woolley at the best of times. She suddenly panicked. Perhaps he'd changed his mind and was going to offer to sell the paper after all? She needn't have worried.

"I bumped into Campbell Lowrie earlier this evening and he told me how well you'd done with the Colonel Lyttleton story. The colonel is an old friend of mine . . ."

"Isn't everyone, Mr Woolley?"

"Pardon?"

"I'm sorry, Mr Woolley, I just meant that you had an amazing circle of friends."

"Yes, well, anyway, I rang the colonel and he said he was very impressed with the sensitive way you handled the questions."

"That was very nice of him. He was terribly co-operative and I hope talking about it helped him a little."

"Oh, it did. It did, Elizabeth."

Elizabeth was holding her breath now, frightened to believe that Jack Woolley was about to offer her the reporter's job she wanted so much. If he did, she might just have to explode with delight. The suspense was killing. Why couldn't he just spit it out? She should have known better. He seldom used one word when two would do.

"You know you mentioned the old agricultural correspondent's job?"

Elizabeth groaned inwardly. Her brother David had managed to persuade Helen Stevenson that she didn't really want to be stuck on agriculture all the time. She wouldn't be best pleased with the offer now being put on the table . . . but if that was the price to be paid for Elizabeth becoming a journalist, she'd understand.

"Yes, I know I mentioned it once or twice but . . ."

"Once or twice? Elizabeth, you've been going on about it for weeks and now I'm totally convinced that it should be reinstated and, what's more, Campbell Lowrie concurs with me."

Elizabeth could see little hope of saving her friend from a fate worse than silage-making, although she was prepared to try.

"But are you sure the farmers around here would accept a woman nosing around their business?"

"That's not fair, Elizabeth. I don't think you can accuse the men around here of being male chauvinists. We're all very fair-minded."

Elizabeth sensed a lost cause.

"What if Helen doesn't want the job?"

"Helen? Helen who? What are you talking about Elizabeth?"

"Helen Stevenson . . . the girl I've been trying to persuade you to make agricultural correspondent. Only to be perfectly honest, Mr Woolley, I'm not sure she still wants it."

Jack Woolley roared with laughter.

"You don't understand, Elizabeth. It's not Helen Stevenson I'm talking about. I know she's perfectly happy where she is. It's you I'm offering the job. It's you I want as agricultural correspondent for the *Echo*!"